P9-CQF-814

This month, in

TALL, DARK...AND FRAMED?
by Cathleen Galitz...

Meet Sebastian Wescott—
millionaire CEO of Wescott Oil...and
a *murderer?* Susan Wysocki, his new attorney,
was determined to prove that Seb was innocent,
but the sexy lawyer just might find *herself* guilty—
of losing her heart to her client!

**SILHOUETTE DESIRE
IS PROUD TO PRESENT THE**

Five wealthy Texas bachelors—all members of
the state's most exclusive club—set out to
uncover the traitor in their midst...
and find true love.

* * *

And don't miss
THE PLAYBOY MEETS HIS MATCH
by Sara Orwig,
The fourth installment of the
Texas Cattleman's Club: The Last Bachelor series.
Available next month in Silhouette Desire!

Dear Reader,

Welcome to Silhouette Desire, where you can spice up your April with six passionate, powerful and provocative romances!

Beloved author Diana Palmer delivers a great read with *A Man of Means,* the latest in her LONG, TALL TEXANS miniseries, as a saucy cook tames a hot-tempered cowboy with her biscuits. Then, enjoy reading how one woman's orderly life is turned upside down when she is wooed by *Mr. Temptation,* April's MAN OF THE MONTH and the first title in Cait London's hot new HEARTBREAKERS miniseries.

Reader favorite Maureen Child proves a naval hero is no match for a determined single mom in *The SEAL's Surrender,* the latest DYNASTIES: THE CONNELLYS title. And a reluctant widow gets a second chance at love in *Her Texan Tycoon* by Jan Hudson.

The drama continues in the TEXAS CATTLEMAN'S CLUB: THE LAST BACHELOR continuity series with *Tall, Dark...and Framed?* by Cathleen Galitz, when an attractive defense attorney falls head over heels for her client— a devastatingly handsome tycoon with a secret. And discover what a ranch foreman, a virgin and her protective brothers have in common in *One Wedding Night...* by Shirley Rogers.

Celebrate the season by pampering yourself with all six of these exciting new love stories.

Enjoy!

Joan Marlow Golan

Joan Marlow Golan
Senior Editor, Silhouette Desire

Please address questions and book requests to:
Silhouette Reader Service
U.S.: 3010 Walden Ave., P.O. Box 1325, Buffalo, NY 14269
Canadian: P.O. Box 609, Fort Erie, Ont. L2A 5X3

Tall, Dark...and Framed?

CATHLEEN GALITZ

Silhouette® Desire®

Published by Silhouette Books

America's Publisher of Contemporary Romance

If you purchased this book without a cover you should be aware
that this book is stolen property. It was reported as "unsold and
destroyed" to the publisher, and neither the author nor the
publisher has received any payment for this "stripped book."

Special thanks and acknowledgment are given to
Cathleen Galitz for her contribution to the
TEXAS CATTLEMAN'S CLUB:
THE LAST BACHELOR series.

To Dixie, Peggy, Jackie and especially Sara,
for taking me under her wing. It has been an honor
working with such talented writers.

SILHOUETTE BOOKS

ISBN 0-373-76433-2

TALL, DARK...AND FRAMED?

Copyright © 2002 by Harlequin Books S.A.

All rights reserved. Except for use in any review, the reproduction
or utilization of this work in whole or in part in any form by any
electronic, mechanical or other means, now known or hereafter
invented, including xerography, photocopying and recording, or in
any information storage or retrieval system, is forbidden without
the written permission of the editorial office, Silhouette Books,
300 East 42nd Street, New York, NY 10017 U.S.A.

All characters in this book have no existence outside the imagination of
the author and have no relation whatsoever to anyone bearing the same
name or names. They are not even distantly inspired by any individual
known or unknown to the author, and all incidents are pure invention.

This edition published by arrangement with Harlequin Books S.A.

® and TM are trademarks of Harlequin Books S.A., used under license.
Trademarks indicated with ® are registered in the United States Patent
and Trademark Office, the Canadian Trade Marks Office and in other
countries.

Visit Silhouette at www.eHarlequin.com

Printed in U.S.A.

Books by Cathleen Galitz

Silhouette Desire

The Cowboy Takes a Bride #1271
Wyoming Cinderella #1373
Her Boss's Baby #1396
Tall, Dark...and Framed? #1433

Silhouette Romance

The Cowboy Who Broke the Mold #1257
100% Pure Cowboy #1279
Wyoming Born & Bred #1381

CATHLEEN GALITZ,

a Wyoming native, teaches English in grades 6-12 in a
rural school that houses kindergartners and seniors in the
same building. She feels blessed to have married a man
who is both supportive and patient. When she's not busy
writing, teaching or chauffeuring her sons to and from
various activities, she can most likely be found indulging
in her favorite pastime—reading.

"What's Happening in Royal?"

NEWS FLASH, April—One of Royal's sexiest bachelors has been arrested…for murder! His friends at the Texas Cattleman's Club and Wescott employees we interviewed all agree that while drop-dead gorgeous Sebastian Wescott might be guilty of breaking the hearts of eligible females everywhere, he couldn't possibly be guilty of *murder!*

In fact, it looks like Sebastian may be breaking one more heart—rumor has it that Seb and his lady lawyer may be spending more time in the *bedroom* than the courtroom! Attorney Susan Wysocki has offered no comment to our reporters, other than her conviction that Sebastian is innocent. So what *really* happened that night? If Sebastian isn't the murderer, why can't he provide an alibi?

Folks in Royal are more than a little disappointed that this year's social event of the season— the Texas Cattleman's Club Ball—has been indefinitely postponed. Members of the club have decided to wait until after Sebastian's trial before they consider rescheduling. Things at the club are looking a little grim these days…especially since the last bachelor standing may be behind bars!

Prologue

"Sebastian Wescott has been arrested."

The news spread through the Texas Cattleman's Club like a wildfire devouring prairie grasslands during a season of drought. Muted whispers set in motion beneath an array of mounted glassy-eyed animal heads grew in intensity until the gleaming Tiffany chandeliers overhead nearly shook from the force of its membership's outrage. It didn't take long for a select group to abandon games of poker and pool where enormous sums of money were at stake to make their way quietly into one of the tasteful private meeting rooms at the back of the club. Here behind closed doors where the lingering odor of expensive cigars was less noticeable, discussions of the most serious nature took place.

A silver samovar with piping hot coffee stood untouched beside a set of fine bone china embossed with the club's distinctive crest. Nothing less than hard liquor was warranted as the rumors resonated from room to spacious room in the nearly one-hundred-year-old building. Members in this time-honored, elite institution were more than social acquaintances. Few would have guessed from its modest exterior that the club was actually a front for a prestigious social enclave working on covert missions. Placed in situations in which the members were often forced to rely on one another for their very lives, they considered themselves closer than actual blood brothers.

Word of Sebastian's disgrace hit everybody hard.

His own half brother, Dorian, appeared inconsolable as he related to the group the events leading up to Seb's arrest. It was no secret to anyone there that Dorian had been deeply worried about Sebastian for the past several weeks. His concern had been the topic of conversation on more than one occasion and had been so overdone that it had put some of the members off. The club was a place where they came to relax at the end of a stressful day, not to wallow in unsubstantiated gossip about one of their own.

Only now it appeared Dorian's fears were not unfounded.

"If only there were some way of helping Sebastian without somehow jeopardizing the anonymity of the club," lamented William Bradford. As Sebastian's partner at Wescott Oil Enterprises, he was fiercely protective not just of the business they ran together but also of his old friend Jack Wescott's son.

"Sebastian says he was out of town on business

the night Eric Chambers was murdered, but I understand he refuses to provide his attorney with an alibi,'' Dorian interjected, anxiety deeply etched on features that reminded everyone present of his half brother.

It was only at Sebastian's insistence that the members of the club had unanimously inducted Dorian a short time ago. As a full-fledged member, he was privy to the workings of their brotherhood, but he hadn't been there long enough to have knowledge of the details regarding the daring missions that sometimes called club members away for indeterminate lengths of time.

It was all Jason Windover, the retired CIA agent, could do to refrain from explaining to this ninny that Sebastian often used his business as a cover. He had been wary of Dorian from the start, and time, unfortunately, hadn't improved his first impression of the man. In fact, Jason had only reluctantly agreed to participate in Dorian's induction ceremony as a favor to Sebastian. Not wanting to endanger a friendship that spanned so many years, he had set aside his misgivings and gone along with his friend's request without giving voice to his qualms.

Jason supposed his suspicions stemmed from his background as an agent. Looking at Dorian now, it was certainly hard to doubt the sincerity of his feelings.

''I say the least we can do is put up his bail,'' William Bradford suggested, not bothering to clear up any misconceptions Dorian might have about his brother's whereabouts on the night in question. ''It's best if no money from Wescott Oil Enterprises is involved, since those funds are under such intense scrutiny at the present.''

Dorian gasped as William's intention dawned on him. ''Are you suggesting that we somehow come up with half a million dollars in bail money between us?''

''Pocket change,'' exclaimed Keith Owen. As the owner of a computer-software firm, he didn't so much as blink at the amount mentioned. ''Count me in.''

''Me, too,'' Jason said. As rich as Midas, he would have given everything he owned to support his old friend.

When Dorian sputtered in disbelief at their overwhelming generosity, they assured him that no one was taking an actual risk with their money. No one among them believed Sebastian would forfeit bond by running out on them. For that matter, no one doubted his innocence.

Lamenting that he personally had little money to put up, Dorian told them all, ''I wish there was more I could do. I wish I could have somehow convinced that hotheaded brother of mine not to try solving his problems all by himself. Well, you all know how he is—so worried about depending on others. He'd rather take matters into his own hands than accept help from calmer heads even when the situation demands it. Lately he's been more short-tempered and violent than usual. I swear if I didn't know better, I might be tempted to believe that—''

Dorian stopped in midsentence as if realizing that he may have said more than he intended. He had the grace to look ashamed.

"I apologize for rambling on like this," he told the men assembled in the room. "It's just that I've been so worried, I guess—"

Eager to put an end to the conversation, Jason interrupted and quickly changed the subject. "No apology necessary. Unfortunately there is one item of business that we can't continue to ignore. Considering that the organizer of our annual Cattleman's Club Charity Ball is under arrest, I think it best if we simply cancel this year's bash altogether."

No amount of alcohol could wash away the bad taste that announcement left in everyone's mouth. Aside from the fact that some very worthy charity would be adversely affected by this vote, none of the men assembled wanted to tell their wives and sweethearts that they were responsible for canceling *the* event of the year. The number of places in Royal where designer evening gowns and diamonds were standard dress was limited, and the ladies were sure to be disappointed. It was a point not lost on William. As the first member out of the five friends who had made the bet to succumb to the allure of marriage, he didn't fancy the idea of breaking the news to his lovely new wife. After enduring a period of restricted confinement to keep her safe, Diana had really been looking forward to this year's ball. With so many club members attending, Will had figured the ball would be a safe enough event for Diana to attend.

"Heck of a way for Seb to avoid paying up on his bet," Keith volunteered, hoping to lighten the mood.

Of all those present when Sebastian posed his now infamous bet about who would be the last bachelor standing at the ball in question, only three remained in the running.

"You would have lost, anyway," Jason told him. Recognized as the club's premier playboy, he had no plans of ever tying himself down.

The ensuing bantering lacked the usual lightheartedness. The thought of Sebastian behind bars put a definite damper on what had started out as a pleasant evening. Beyond posting bail as quickly as possible, there was little any of them could do to help their old friend besides pray.

Each did pray in his own private way, passing one by one beneath the iron-studded sign that hung over the entrance door. It proclaimed the club's motto for all to see: *Leadership, Justice and Peace.* Men willing to risk their own lives to promote those ideals were at a loss as to how to help one of their own.

Perhaps, Jason mused, *Faith* would have to be added to that venerable old sign.

One

Sebastian Wescott looked around the drab law office and shook his head in dismay. Why his half brother would even consider such a second-rate firm was beyond him. He supposed it either had something to do with the petite pretty blonde sitting across the desk from him or Dorian's grudging attitude toward money. Having grown up without it, Dorian was still uncomfortable with the thought of spending vast sums of money when one could get an item of comparable value at a blue-light special. As touching as Dorian's gesture was in providing Susan Wysocki a modest retainer out of his own pocket, Sebastian wasn't at all happy with shopping discount when it came to legal representation.

Especially when his own life and freedom were at stake.

Coming here at all had been against his better judgment. Dorian practically had to drag him here by force. Perched on the edge of the chair next to his own, his half brother looked like he was considering blocking the door to prevent Sebastian from leaving before hearing this lawyer out. If he had been more like his old man, Sebastian would simply have twisted a couple of arms and paid off the judge to prevent this case from ever going to trial. But ever since he was a boy, Sebastian had done everything in his power to ensure he was nothing like his ruthless father. Even after going into the family business and becoming outrageously successful in his own right, he could still feel the cold breath of his father's ghost on the back of his neck.

His deep-seated need to separate himself from Jack Wescott was partially responsible for his membership in the Texas Cattleman's Club. The state's most exclusive fraternity boasted a men-only membership of the richest, most established echelon in the Lone Star State. Few people knew that behind the club's elegant, polished facade was a secret organization so select, its members could work covertly to protect the lives of the innocent. When they weren't involved in secret missions, the membership focused their collective energy on keeping their bustling West Texas hometown prosperous and civic-minded.

It wasn't the sort of organization that Jack Wescott would ever have been invited to join. Jack's idea of a secret mission was sneaking off to the Pussy Cat Club some fifty miles away. Indeed, Jack had been a man far more interested in pursuing his own twisted desires than in being a father to his children, both those sired within and outside the sacred bonds of marriage.

A fact not lost on poor Dorian, who showed up on Sebastian's doorstep one fine day not so very long ago claiming they were blood kin. According to Dorian, his mother had given him up for adoption when Jack Wescott refused to acknowledge him as a son and declared that he wasn't about to provide a single penny of child support. It wasn't until Jack's death that Dorian's birth mother looked up her son and informed him that the wealthy industrialist who'd just died was actually his father.

Had Sebastian had more faith in his father and had Dorian not borne such a striking resemblance to himself, he might well have sent the stranger packing and washed his hands of the whole sordid matter. Instead, he again felt bound to atone for his father's sins.

As it turned out, giving Dorian a job in computer services at Wescott Oil had been one good deed that had truly come full circle. If anyone had ever suggested to Sebastian that his long-lost brother would be the first to rush to his defense at the lowest point in Sebastian's life, he would have called him crazy. Recalling the parable about the poor widow giving her last few coins to charity, he wished there was some way of refusing his brother's gift without seeming ungrateful.

Without somehow offending him.

The circumstances surrounding the accusations leveled at Sebastian only added to his frustration and rage. Aside from a burning desire to clear his good name and secure his independence, he was determined to find out who had murdered his colleague, in the process framing Sebastian for the heinous deed. He vowed the killer would pay dearly for his treachery.

"This is utterly idiotic!" he shouted, landing a large fist upon the desk and causing the woman behind it to jump in alarm. "I don't need a lawyer. I'm innocent!"

As a wolf in sheep's clothing, Susan thought wryly.

"That is exactly the reason you need my services, Mr. Wescott," she assured him with cool poise intended to mask her own misgivings.

The truth was, if the opportunity to represent the virile man sitting on the other side of her desk hadn't been so crucial to her financial survival, Susan Wysocki would likely have handed back the substantial retainer Dorian Brady had given her and run as fast as possible in the opposite direction.

For starters, Sebastian Wescott reminded her a little too much of her ex-husband. He was that sure of himself. Not that Joe had been anywhere near as physically imposing as this man. Truly Sebastian was nothing short of feral in the way he dominated the room. Not even the most expensive, hand-tailored suit in the world could hide a masculine physique that suggested the power and ferocity of a sleek panther.

A sleek, *caged* panther, she mentally amended.

Every so often her would-be client jumped out of his chair, paced back and forth in front of her scarred oak desk and punctuated the air with another gesture of pure outrage. It was all Susan could do to keep from leaning back in her chair to distance herself from his anger.

At the same time, it was all she could do to keep from leaning toward him as if pulled by a magnet.

She made a mental note to load the jury with women if this case ever actually went to trial. No matter how strong the prosecution's case, they wouldn't stand a chance if the jury happened to fall in love with the sexy millionaire accused of murdering his associate Eric Chambers, vice president of accounting for Wescott Oil.

She also didn't like the way those silver-gray eyes of his made her go all shivery inside whenever he stopped in the midst of his pacing to train them on her. It was difficult to keep from squirming beneath his scrutiny. Susan's body was still tingling from the perfunctory handshake they'd exchanged when Sebastian had first introduced himself. She assumed that the electrical current that held her as immobile as if she'd embraced a live wire was simply her body's way of warning her of impending danger.

Painful past experience had taught her to trust her gut feelings.

She had been relieved when Sebastian had finally released that all-too-masculine grip. At thirty, she wasn't so naive that she didn't recognize her reaction for what it was—lust, in its most primitive and dangerous form. Fearing the same kind of machismo that had initially attracted her to her ex-husband, Susan reminded herself that finding the right man was a matter of choice better left to a level head than to fickle hormones.

It was unfortunate that Sebastian's half brother, Dorian Brady, wasn't more her type. He impressed her as being far less edgy than his sibling. Though strikingly similar in appearance to his brother, Dorian's appeal was subtler, Susan decided. He was smaller in stature, but his eyes were nearly the same astonishing shade of silver as Sebastian's. However, for some unfathomable reason, his gaze did not immediately hold her an unwilling captive the way Sebastian's did. There was a swaggering seductiveness in Sebastian's demeanor that contrasted sharply with his brother's more understated nature.

That her body didn't react in such openly traitorous ways to Dorian was definitely part of his charm to the wary Susan. Once burned... She cut off the thought and concentrated on the legal matter at hand.

Having received an abbreviated version from Dorian of how he had only a short time ago come to locate his long-lost family, Susan wasn't quite sure exactly how his relationship with Sebastian stood. Other than the fact that Dorian seemed to hold no malice toward his half brother, who had been born with a silver spoon in his mouth. By his own account, Dorian—who had been abandoned by Sebastian's philandering father and put up for adoption by his brokenhearted mother—could barely afford plastic cutlery while growing up. That he had paid Susan's retainer out of his own pocket, insisting on providing legal representation for his mulish kin, spoke volumes about him. Such loyalty was rare even among siblings raised together from birth. Susan could only assume that being new in town, Dorian knew nothing of her recent string of bad luck.

Losing two close court cases in a row had done more than simply damage her self-esteem. The lack of clients beating down her door was mute testimony of her own dwindling faith in her skills as an attorney. Her once-upon-a-time dream of giving the little guy a voice in the legal system—the same dream that had kept her going throughout law school—was now strained by the necessity of simply supporting herself.

Hadn't Joe warned her that she didn't stand a chance of making it on her own? He'd predicted that without his money and influence, she would fold like a house of cards....

Gritting her teeth at the memory of her ex-husband's parting shot, Susan bolstered her flagging confidence with the desire to prove him wrong. Believing that success would ultimately prove the sweetest revenge, she smiled confidently at the intimidating Mr. Wescott and offered him a cup of coffee. He declined with nothing more than a terse shake of his head.

Trying to calm this man down was like convincing a wild animal to step willingly into a cage.

With her.

Armed with nothing but bravado and determination, Susan assessed her options. Though female intuition warned her to stay far, far away from Sebastian Wescott, she desperately needed just such an incredible opportunity. A high-profile case like this could well be her ticket to a recovery that would be as much emotional as financial for her. No matter how much working with this man might stir a prickly feminine responsiveness that was best left sleeping, it certainly beat chasing ambulances—which was where she feared she was headed if business didn't pick up soon.

In fact, if things didn't pick up, Susan feared she might have to lay off her secretary, Ann Worthe. A single mother who had just left an abusive marriage herself, Ann would be as devastated as Susan by such an unfortunate turn of events. Not only wouldn't she be able to continue the night classes she was taking in hopes of becoming a paralegal, Ann would have trouble feeding her three young children without the help of food stamps—something the proud young mother had vowed never to do. Aside from the heart-wrenching personal aspects of laying off a woman she considered a friend, Susan knew such a move would mark the end of her own hard-fought dreams and aspirations. There was simply no way she could do her job as a lawyer and manage the office at the same time.

Landing the case of such a prominent citizen as Sebastian Wescott would certainly bolster her standing in the legal community. Lately she had been feeling like the local pariah among the elite of Royal, many of whom were aligned with her influential ex-husband and appeared to relish her past few defeats in the courtroom. The thought of seeing those good old Texas boys, some of whom openly believed the law was best left to men alone, turn pea green with envy was enough to straighten her spine.

Now was not the time to let silly girlish palpitations interfere with good sense. Just because her mind kept wandering to thoughts of how Sebastian might look naked in her bed didn't mean anything would ever come of such outlandish fantasies. Aside from the fact that Sebastian Wescott could have any woman he wanted, the realization that he was accused of murder should have been more than enough to cool her blood. But it continued to course through her veins in hot, pounding spurts of female awareness.

Nonetheless, by the time Sebastian stopped pacing and took his seat again, Susan had made up her mind. If by some miracle, she could actually convince this millionaire oil baron that she was the best lawyer for the job, she would represent him as if more than just *his* life was on the line.

In a manner of speaking, hers was, too.

"Now that you're sitting down, let me assure you that I am more than capable and willing to take your case on and I will focus 110% of my time and energy on your behalf."

Sebastian was caught off guard by the haunting feminine quality of the voice that entreated him to remain calm. What was it about that particular inflection that wound its way around every nerve ending in his body and made him ache with an unfamiliar longing?

Searching for the answer to that particular question in a pair of mesmerizing hazel eyes was not a wise choice, he decided. Blue? Gray? Green? He could no more get a fix on their exact shade than a chameleon could remain satisfied with any one hue. It was his opinion that lawyers with winsome eyes should be permanently disbarred on the basis of unfair practices.

Had Susan Wysocki somehow hypnotized him into actually considering adding her to his already substantial legal team? Not that it really mattered, Sebastian told himself. After all, what was one more attorney's salary to a self-made millionaire?

From the looks of her worn office chair, Susan Wysocki could certainly use the money. Why that mattered to Sebastian was not something he chose to reflect upon for long. He was used to trusting his gut instincts. That for some inexplicable reason he was drawn to this woman was impetus enough for him to set aside his reservations and actually consider hiring her.

Up until now he'd had no reason to keep any criminal lawyers on staff, his need being more in the way of corporate and business strategists. They would be of little use in a courtroom, but he respected their collective opinion nonetheless. Besides, Seb believed that this case would never actually go to trial.

"Mr. Wescott?" Susan repeated, attempting to bring his focus back to what was becoming a distinctly one-sided conversation.

With a start, Sebastian realized that Susan was staring at him as if considering whether to dial 911. He didn't think it prudent to explain that he had been focusing on how the sunlight spilling in through the window cast a halo about her hair. Which was a most extraordinary color. Not a brash store-bought yellow, it was a true blond.

Whiplash blond, his father would have called it.

Like wild, dark honey.

Sebastian wondered if it felt as silky as it looked. This lady didn't seem the type to fix those long, soft curls with half a can of hairspray every day to achieve the "big hair" that Texan women made famous. Having endured the coquettish advances of countless such polished vixens, he was struck by the fact that Susan Wysocki seemed singularly unaware of her natural beauty. He wondered if she even considered what an asset her looks would be in the courtroom.

"Are you all right, Mr. Wescott?" she asked, genuine concern etching worry lines upon her countenance.

"Call me Seb," he said, shaking his head to rid it of the cobwebs. "My friends do."

"I'd like that," Susan replied, keenly aware that her pulse had pole-vaulted at the sound of the shortened, softer name and the glib invitation into his elite circle of friends.

Her response couldn't have been more genuine. As long as they could maintain a friendly relationship, Susan was fairly certain there would be no problem representing this man. As a friend, Sebastian Wescott was bound to be a powerful and affluent ally. As a lover, she suspected he would be as dangerous to a woman's heart as an arrow dipped in poison. As an enemy, he was probably deadly.

Susan quickly amended that particular choice of words, fearing it might color her perception of whether Sebastian Wescott was actually capable of the crime of which he was accused. But before she could ascertain anything so monumental, she needed to figure out a way to get her own capricious hormones under control. Right now the way this man was looking at her was making her feel hot all over.

Decidedly uncomfortable.

And every bit a woman.

She blinked hard. Twice. Then finally succumbed to the urge to turn her gaze to the floor, where she pretended to study the toes of her sensible navy pumps. Susan knew herself to be plain and unsophisticated compared to the kind of women "Seb" was used to.

Seeing the flicker of pain in Susan's eyes, Seb felt a protective pang deep in his heart. A heart some people liked to think was as hard and black as his father's, but in truth was much more susceptible to weakness. As much as this woman wanted to come across as some stereotypical thick-skinned lawyer, he recognized the vulnerability she was trying so hard to hide.

And was drawn to it like a moth to a flame.

As a member of the Texas Cattleman's Club, he had pledged his very life to protecting innocents. The innately honest aura surrounding this woman stirred his sense of old-fashioned chivalry—which struck him as ironic, considering that at the moment *she* was the one offering to save *him*. Seb was surprised by the intensity of the protective instincts welling up inside him. He didn't hold lawyers in high esteem. As a rule, he thought them far more concerned about lining their own pockets than in genuinely pursuing justice. For some reason he couldn't bring himself to lump this fascinating blond creature in with such parasites.

He suspected Susan Wysocki would be shocked to discover they had much in common. *Leadership, Justice and Peace* were the words burned into an iron-studded plaque hung in a place of honor at the Texas Cattleman's Club. More than just a motto, they were the tenets by which the members lived. Even if Seb were to allow this lovely lady to represent him in a court of law, he doubted whether she would be able to understand that, come what may, he was duty bound to keep his whereabouts the night of the murder a secret. Protecting the club and the nature of the assignment that had taken him away that night was every bit as important as protecting his own life.

If it wasn't, this would be an open-and-shut case, and he could merrily go on with life as he knew it without so much as missing a beat.

And he would never have had the chance to make the lovely Ms. Wysocki's acquaintance and become so enamored by her amazing hazel eyes. It was the only upside Seb could find to the miserable predicament in which he was mired. That she was trying to hide the nervous flutter of her hands by rearranging a stack of papers on an otherwise clean desk struck him as inexplicably endearing. He noticed that her left hand was devoid of a wedding ring.

In light of the fact that the chemistry between them was anything but businesslike, Susan's prim and proper attitude seemed utterly incongruent. Women threw themselves at Seb all the time. Oddly enough, none of their bold sexual advances had half the effect on him as had Susan's simple handshake. Accompanied as it was by the widening of those big hazel eyes, he knew for a fact that she had felt something, too.

Like a tremor.

The kind that precedes an earthquake.

And changes one's life forever.

Indeed, fate's little aftershocks were still playing havoc with rational thought. Surely that alone caused the words to tumble out of his mouth of their own volition.

"If you'd like to go over the particulars of the case, I'll be glad to meet with you later this evening—at my place, over drinks."

Given the condition of her office furniture, Seb would have expected Susan to jump at the opportunity to make some real money. Thus, her reaction to his invitation both surprised and disconcerted him. That she appeared less than thrilled at the prospect of spending the evening with him was an understatement. She looked downright aghast.

Something both scared and needy glistening in those hypnotic eyes was all that kept him from being insulted by her lack of enthusiasm.

"Seb," she said in her most coolly detached lawyer voice, all the while the intimacy of his pet name on her tongue sending a delicious shiver up her spine. "Surely you understand that I have to maintain a professional relationship with all my clients."

Unused to being rebuffed, Seb was quick to make light of her presumption. "Were you thinking along any other lines, Ms. Wysocki?" he taunted. "I have a meeting later this afternoon at the Cattleman's Club that I can't miss. This evening is the only time I have to go over the specifics of the case. That is, if you're still interested in representing me."

If she was still interested!

Only a crazy woman would turn down an offer like this one on any level—professional or romantic—though Susan knew she had ruined any chances of the latter with her uptight reproach to a simple request for an after-hours meeting. Seb's straightforward response had left her feeling like a complete idiot. Lord knows, she had worked around other clients' schedules on more than one occasion.

Susan was spared an immediate response by the timeliness of Dorian's interruption. For a moment she had almost forgotten he was in the room with them. Clearly thrilled that his big brother was actually considering accepting his gift of her legal services, he jumped into the conversation feetfirst. "If you'd be more comfortable with me present, Ms. Wysocki, I'd be glad to be there, as well."

It was all Susan could do to keep from rolling her eyes. Dorian must have read the hesitancy in her body language and come to the conclusion that she was frightened of being alone with Seb. He was right, of course, but not for any of the reasons she suspected were running through his mind at the moment. For heaven's sake, she was no shy virgin afraid of being compromised by a big bad wolf lurking in the woods. As much as she appreciated Dorian's concern, she did not need his protection. Even though Sebastian was accused of murder, she certainly didn't get any creepy vibes from him. If the truth were known, she suspected that more women accosted *him* than the other way around. Many of her own girlfriends would undoubtedly claw their way around her for the opportunity to spend an evening alone with such a man.

What Susan was really afraid of was her own reaction to being alone with a man who, by his very

presence, reminded her that beneath her professional
pin-striped suit jacket beat the heart of a woman very
much longing for more than business aspirations to
fill the void in her life.

"That won't be necessary," Seb assured Dorian
with a black glare that lingered long enough for him
to get the hint.

"Oh, I forgot," Dorian exclaimed, snapping his
fingers and donning a hearty grin. "I have someplace
to be tonight, too. Wouldn't want to break the little
lady's heart by standing her up, you know."

Susan winced. The ploy was so patently obvious
that she couldn't help but wonder why she had ever
thought Dorian subtle. Clearly he was more enamored of the prospect of pleasing Sebastian than he
was of her. Not that he shouldn't feel more allegiance
to a brother than a complete stranger, she reminded
herself.

Susan wished she could rationalize away her fears
as easily. Maybe Sebastian really did have a meeting
at the Texas Cattleman's Club. Maybe it really was
more important than clearing his name of murder.
And maybe she was imagining that predatory interest
in his eyes. All Susan knew for sure was that such
heavy-handed tactics were reminiscent of the way
her ex-husband used to manipulate her.

She smiled sweetly at her new client, the one who
just might be the answer to her prayers if she played
her cards right. Reminding herself that she was indeed a big girl and capable of separating past hurts
from present opportunities, she tamped down her re-
sentments. As long as she promised not to involve

her heart in the case, there was really no reason to turn good fortune away from her doorstep.

"What time do you want me to be there?" she asked.

Two

It seemed fitting that Susan arrive at Sebastian Wescott's estate on April Fools' Day. She felt very foolish indeed waiting for the heavy wrought-iron gates to swing open and admit her. Feeling rather as if she should be placing an order at a fast-food joint, she spoke into the intercom to announce herself. A few minutes later she was parking her late-model Taurus behind a shiny new Porsche and making her way to the front door of a truly magnificent home. For a minute there she'd been afraid a valet was going to rush out and tell her to move "that piece of junk."

Unlike Jack Wescott's stone mansion, which was prominently displayed atop a hill overlooking Royal, his son's ranch was more secluded and, Susan observed, far less ostentatious. A stately driveway wound its way through parklike acres of manicured lawns and mature trees. Redbrick privacy walls beckoned visitors to enjoy the world of the privileged, if only for a short time. Sebastian's home itself was a country-style Georgian colonial, white with dark-green eaves, tiles and shutters. One could catch only a glimpse of the tennis courts, swimming pools and stables tucked neatly behind the spacious home. How a multimillion-dollar estate managed to exude an air of country coziness was enough to make Susan give silent praise to the architect who had designed it.

Wiping her palms on the front of her demure navy suit, she waited for the butler to open the door. She was surprised when she was greeted by Sebastian himself, wearing a comfortable pair of blue jeans and a sweatshirt. The smile on his face did nothing to lessen the impact of his devastating good looks, which had haunted her ever since he'd stepped foot in her office earlier in the day.

"Come on in," Sebastian bid her with a familiarity she found somehow both engaging and unsettling.

If only she could get her pulse rate up this easily at her weekly aerobic workouts! Feeling the need to steady herself, Susan stopped a moment to lean against the doorway and check her watch, vowing to give this heartbreaker no more than a couple of hours of her precious time before skedaddling back to the safety of her modest, decidedly middle-class apartment. As tempting as it might be to indulge in little-girl fantasies, she didn't need to remind herself that she hadn't been summoned to Prince Charming's fancy ball. Nor did she intend to leave any glass slipper behind at the stroke of midnight. Undeniably, one thing marriage to Joe had taught her was to look for the tarnish on any supposed knight's gleaming armor. That Sebastian was facing charges for a heinous crime should have been more than enough to take the shine off *his* armor, were it the brightest sterling silver.

"I hope you haven't eaten yet," Sebastian said. "I just put steaks for two on the grill."

The heavenly smells wafting through the house brought back the inadequacy of Susan's dinner to her with a swiftness that overpowered her senses. The peanut-butter sandwich she had washed down earlier with a glass of milk while poring over her law books had done little to satisfy her appetite.

"Thank you, but I've already eaten," she told him stiffly.

It was difficult to sound convincing over the rumbling of her stomach.

The sound caused Sebastian to quirk an eyebrow at her, but he gallantly refrained from making comment. Instead, he proceeded to lead her through the dining room at such a fast clip that Susan barely had time to appreciate the elegance of a room flanked by high-arched windows and vaulted ceilings. Grabbing an apron off the back of a white leather couch, Sebastian invited her to follow him through a set of open French doors onto the patio, where smoke was leaking around the edges of a barbecue grill. Slipping an oven mitt on one hand, he opened the lid and began attacking a couple of thick steaks with a pair of long-handled tongs.

"Don't worry. I have everything under control," Sebastian hastened to assure her.

Indeed, the man did give the appearance that nothing at all in his life was amiss. The scene had such a homey feel to it that Susan was tempted to kick off her high heels, dangle her tired feet over the side of an Olympic-size swimming pool and ask her client if he could spare a beer. As Sebastian struggled to get the steaks onto a platter and extinguish a flame that had gotten almost out of control during his absence, Susan felt a giggle gurgling up from somewhere inside her. As much as she hated to admit it, the truth was she had rather expected an envoy of well-trained servants to be waiting hand and foot on their playboy master. A man who, with a subtle gesture, would have his staff dimming the lights before vacating the premises to allow him to have his way with yet another defenseless maiden hoping to lay claim to a portion of his fortune.

"What's so funny?" Sebastian asked, shutting off the grill and making his way to her side.

He set the heavy platter down on a round patio table and proceeded to adjust the sturdy yellow umbrella that shot out of its center like a sunflower. Susan was glad that its position blocked only the glare and not the view of a magnificent sunset. Beyond the lush grounds lay the Texas desert, equally breathtaking in its stark beauty. A profusion of bluebonnets, the state flower—named by pioneer women reminded of their own simple head coverings—draped the desert in bolts of bright homespun calico.

"You," she replied succinctly, giving him the first genuine smile she'd been able to locate all day long.

What she would have given for the experience of coming home to find Joe wearing such domestic garb. To the best of her recollection, the closest her ex-husband had come to donning an apron was when he brushed against it hanging up in the pantry while searching for a bottle of cognac.

"I have to admit I never imagined this meeting occurring with you in an apron."

Sebastian didn't seem to take offense. "And just what *did* you think I'd be wearing?" he asked.

Susan noticed how his friendly expression softened the angular cut of his jaw.

"A smoking jacket, I suppose. An imported red-silk one that your manservant helped you into," she replied with a blush that threatened to match the sunset in all its flaming glory.

Feigning regret, he shook his head at her. "It's not often that I'm mistaken for Bruce Wayne. I hope you're not disappointed that Robin can't make it tonight and that the Bat Cave is closed for repairs."

Susan couldn't refrain from smiling at the witty remark.

"A smile does nice things for your face," Seb commented. "You should think of wearing one more often."

"The same goes for you," she replied, recalling the fierce creature who had marched into her office a few short hours ago and left her feeling breathless and a little frightened. On his own turf this man was far less intimidating.

Susan was secretly pleased when Sebastian pulled out the chair for her and bid her to sit down. She appreciated the gesture. It was the kind of simple courtesy that, in her opinion, too many women took for granted.

"Are you sure you aren't the least bit hungry?"
Sebastian asked.

The telltale twinkle in those silver eyes could have
been merely the reflection of light off the pool, but
Susan didn't think so. Drinking in the aroma of juicy
T-bone steaks, she allowed her earlier resolve to dis-
sipate amid the steam of two huge, aluminum-
covered baked potatoes that Sebastian pulled off the
grill and placed beside the platter of meat.

"I suppose I could eat a bite or two—that is, if
you wouldn't mind cutting one of those steaks in two
and saving the rest for later," she suggested, hoping
that her host would give her arm one final tiny twist.

Sebastian hastened to assure her that she should
simply eat as much as she wanted and that he would
give whatever was left over to his dogs, Pal and
Buddy. Since Miss Manners insisted that one
shouldn't speak with a mouthful of delicious food,
Susan was saved from commenting on his dogs'
names, which seemed far too cute for such a macho
man.

Not liking to cook for herself alone, Susan often
grabbed a bite at the local diner, a greasy spoon that
proudly splashed its name across paper place mats:
"The Royal Diner—Food Fit for a King!" Looking
around at her present elegant surroundings, Susan
doubted that Sebastian frequented the place.

When he graciously offered to make her any kind
of drink she wanted from the poolside bar, she primly
declined anything more potent than a cola. It was,
after all, one thing to succumb to hunger pangs and
quite another to compromise her professionalism by
clouding her judgment with alcohol. Furtively eyeing

her client's cold beer, she was relieved to find he wasn't the type who favored drinks with difficult-to-pronounce names in hopes of impressing her. It pleased her to discover that her host wasn't a snob like Joe, who sniffed corks and made a big deal out of knowing the vintage of priceless wines. And, Susan was glad to see that, also unlike Joe, Seb had no problem stopping after one drink.

How easy it had been to slip into the habit of calling this lion of a man by his pet name. Seb certainly suited him better than Sebastian, Susan thought. As she polished off the last bite of a steak she had earlier protested was far too big for her to consume alone, she wondered if Jack Wescott had deliberately chosen the imposing name "Sebastian" for his baby boy, planning to mold his son into a man who would someday take over an empire. Having grown up without the benefits of privilege herself, Susan found it difficult to imagine the woes of a poor little rich boy. Still, the thought that Seb might not have had a picture-perfect childhood bothered her more than it probably should have.

Susan refused to allow such speculative thoughts to darken the luxurious pleasure of a perfect spring evening. As she drank in the fading rays of the setting sun, apprehension slipped from her slender shoulders as easily as her jacket had earlier. It had been far too long since she had last watched the sun bid the day a glorious adieu and paused to appreciate the beauty of the surrounding countryside. Midland was the closest city, and it was a good fifty miles away. The seclusion of this lush estate, surrounded as it was by desert and buffeted by almost unceasing winds, made it seem as if Royal itself was equally distant.

''A girl could get used to this kind of treatment,'' Susan admitted, feeling as if she was dropping in on a mirage. With a satisfied sigh, she pushed herself away from the table and announced that the evening was growing cool and it was time to get down to business.

Though Seb grimaced, he dutifully rose to his feet and began clearing the table. Susan followed his lead.

''My housekeeper, Rosa, would have my hide if I left the dishes outside overnight,'' he explained with a touch of chagrin.

Happy to pitch in, Susan was impressed both with the clout Rosa wielded over her employer and with Seb's willingness to do what she assumed most millionaires would find beneath their dignity. The easy banter that accompanied them into the kitchen seemed somehow incongruent in their surroundings. The latest in kitchen appliances sparkled beneath soft lighting, a testament to Rosa's dedication. All that gleaming black-and-white modernism was saved from its usual cold feel by the very same lemony scent that Susan remembered in her own mother's kitchen. One whiff carried her back to a simpler time when she and her five siblings were all crowded together in public housing that offered little in privacy, but much in the way of inspiration nurtured by their parents' dreams of a better life for their children.

Her background had a lot to do with shaping her dream of making life better for other children. Particularly those coping with lack of available and adequate housing, uncooperative slumlords, insufficient food and, God forbid, abusive parents. Folding her dish towel and setting it atop a spotless counter, Susan realized just how far down the road this man's case was from her original goal. Defending millionaires was hardly championing the cause of the poor. In a system in which "justice" too often could be bought, she couldn't help but wonder why someone with Seb's resources would bother taking a chance on her skills as a lawyer.

But reminding herself how desperately she needed to win this case to resuscitate her floundering dream, she refused to second-guess her host. Determined not to look the proverbial gift horse in the mouth, she promised simply do her best and prove herself worthy of Seb's trust.

Citing the need to go to the bathroom, she returned to the kitchen a few moments later carrying her briefcase. "Would it be all right to work in here?" Susan asked, setting it on the table. "Or would you rather we moved into the den?"

"Here is fine," Seb agreed amicably, pulling up a chair to the kitchen table himself.

Susan noticed him looking at the battered leather case and briefly considered explaining that it had been a gift from her parents when she graduated from law school. More than just one of her colleagues had hinted that she should invest in a new briefcase, but this particular one held more than just papers. In it resided her parents' pride and her own aspirations. Every nick and scratch in its surface represented her hard-fought battle for independence. Once she had actually used it as a shield when, in a childish temper tantrum, Joe had thrown his drink across the room at her, demanding she give up this foolishness and drop out of school altogether. As the man of the house, he was deeply insulted that his wife felt the need to contribute financially to their marriage.

Vainly attempting to brush aside the memory, like someone fanning the air to rid it of the lingering smell of cigar smoke, Susan readjusted her professional face before addressing Sebastian again.

"Let's get started then, shall we?"

Pleased that he offered no protest to the suggestion, Susan got down to business. Sunset had reluctantly given way to twilight, and pale purple light filtered in through the windows, reminding Susan of her broken promise to stay but a couple of hours, tops. Taking out a yellow legal pad, she began asking rapid-fire questions.

Pausing a moment to jot down an important note, she told him, "I hope you don't feel like you're being interrogated, but I've got to warn you, this is nothing compared to what the prosecution will do if they ever get you on the stand."

"I expect you to call the shots as you see them, Counselor," Seb assured her.

Warmth flooded through Susan's entire being at the comment. Impressed by the intelligence and charm to which she'd been subjected all evening, she found herself toying with the idea of extending their professional relationship to include a personal friendship. It had been a long time since she'd enjoyed a man's company so much without worrying about whether he was coming on to her.

Not that she would ever expect a man like Sebastian Wescott to consider her anything more than an amusing diversion. Susan didn't doubt that he could have his pick of rich, sophisticated women at the snap of his fingers. But she didn't much cotton to the idea of being the flavor of the month. She reminded herself that it was nothing more than circumstances that had brought them together.

"Are you married?" she asked, starting out with a standard set of questions intended not only to give her necessary background information but also to ease clients into the inquiry process itself. "And do you have any children?"

"No to both questions," Seb replied with a trace of regret in his voice. "Someday if the right woman were to come along, I'd like to remedy that. Nothing could make me happier than to fill this house with the sound of children playing."

It wasn't the response she expected. Susan wondered if Seb noticed that her pen remained poised over her note pad. She could no more make it obey than she could explain why it was suddenly so hard remembering how to breathe.

"How about you?" Seb asked smoothly, switching the topic of conversation from him to her.

Susan swallowed. A private person by nature, she was reticent about sharing personal information with a client. Particularly one accused of murder. Nonetheless, the question was harmless enough, and every good lawyer understood the need to establish rapport with the person he or she was hired to represent.

"Not any more," she answered succinctly, hoping to bring his inquiries to an end with no more explanation than the bare facts.

"Any children?"

"Thankfully no."

Though the words sounded harsh to her own ears, something in the way Seb's eyes softened invitingly encouraged her to continue.

"I've witnessed too many ugly custody battles to believe that children survive unscathed. I don't think it's fair to them."

"I don't, either," Seb replied.

His gaze collided with hers, establishing a tacit understanding that surpassed logical explanation. Susan wondered if his conviction lay in the devastation of living in a broken home as a child himself—or in something far bigger than personal experience alone. She couldn't help but wonder what secrets were hidden in the depths of those arresting gray eyes.

Clicking her pen, she reminded herself that she was not here on a social visit.

"We might as well get down to business," she said, dispensing of any pretense for further conversation outside the bounds of the case at hand. "Let's start by establishing your alibi. Where were you the night of the murder and who would be willing to testify as to your whereabouts?"

"Was your ex-husband fond of children?"

"Only in marketing campaigns promoting any product he was peddling," Susan replied, not missing a beat. "Where exactly did you say you were on the night in question?"

Seb grinned at her, and she caught a glimpse of what he must have looked like as a child with chocolate smeared around his mouth and a cookie jar lid hidden behind his back.

"I didn't. Right now I'm far more interested in

you. It's been a long time since I've had the company of such a fascinating woman. I want to know what makes you tick.''

Caught off guard by his easy flattery, Susan feigned irritation.

''If I indulge your curiosity, can we proceed with the specifics of your case?''

Nodding, Seb smiled at her again. Susan wondered if she should brace herself against the edge of the table for fear of falling completely under his charm. Setting her pen down with a sigh, she propped her elbows on the table instead and cupped her chin in her hands.

''Then by all means, fire away.''

Despite her resolve to cut her answers short, she found herself compelled to respond in more than just the customary, perfunctory manner to the questions he asked. Perhaps it was just a way of paying tribute to his charisma. And to her own loneliness, Susan supposed on some level. It had been so long since anyone had shown any interest in her as a unique and fascinating individual that she was caught off guard by the attention lavished upon her.

There had been no need for Seb to ply her with liquor to get her to divulge more about her own background than she had intended. Merely by being attentive and interested in what she had to say, he gave the impression that he found her bright and funny and captivating. There was no denying that it was flattering. Indeed, such charm would be hard for the most jaded woman to shrug off.

Despite the circumstances that had brought her here, Susan was far from jaded. Somewhere deep inside of her still lived the same little girl who had vowed to make the world a better place through her own sheer determination to put the bad guys behind bars and represent those handsome fellows wearing white cowboy hats.

And yes, she had noticed a cream-colored Stetson dangling from the coatrack in the foyer on her way in.

Fortunately for her own conscience, Susan had become convinced over the course of the evening that, while Sebastian Wescott might well be a brutal businessman when circumstances warranted it, her attractive host was simply incapable of murder. Someone who named his dogs Pal and Buddy and was cowed by his housekeeper simply wasn't capable of the heartlessness necessary to take a human life. Was he?

By the time Susan had exhausted her extensive list of questions, night had fallen. Putting a hand to the small of her back, she stretched her stiff muscles. How inviting that dip in the Jacuzzi sounded when Sebastian offered it, informing her that he had an abundance of swimsuits of all sizes if she happened to be the shy type. The thought of spending any time at all in a hot tub with this magnificent male specimen, whether naked or fully clothed, made her think it would be a whole lot easier to jump into a roaring fire than endure the hot flashes of passion that such images stirred in her.

Feigning a yawn, she said it was past her bedtime. She scheduled their next appointment into her time-planner before allowing him to escort her to her vehicle. Overhead the sky was a canopy of black velvet sprinkled with precious jewels.

"I'm afraid you missed your calling," she said as Seb opened the car door for her.

He looked perplexed. "What do you mean?"

"The way you turned the tables on me tonight and had me answering more questions than you did makes me believe you would have made an excellent lawyer yourself," she clarified.

Sebastian's laugh was a wholesome sound, which echoed off the nearby sand hills and resonated in the chambers of Susan's heart. It had a full-bodied quality that caused her pulse to thrum.

"Is it so hard for you to believe I just might be interested in you, Susan?" he asked, tilting up her chin so that she couldn't avoid looking into his eyes. They were the same astonishing color as the stars above. Liquid and as feral as those of a timber wolf.

When she shivered beneath that predatory gaze, Seb asked if she was cold.

Feeling the warmth of his breath, Susan shook her head. Actually she was feeling oddly flushed. It was as if some secret part of her heart that had been frozen for a long time was beginning to thaw and sending the message to every nerve ending in her body. Tingling all over, she lowered her lashes in anticipation.

In anticipation of what? she wondered dazedly.

A kiss that would violate the sacred bond between a lawyer and client.

Reminding herself that she could scarce afford such a costly mistake, Susan maintained that she could not possibly be so stupid as to fall for another forceful man, cut from the same cloth as the man who had already left permanent scars on her heart. A man so sure of himself that he would rather rely on his own ability to problem-solve than depend on anyone else for help—hence his evasiveness about his whereabouts on the night in question.

A man so clearly protective of vulnerable women like her that some might think it verged on being chauvinistic. And so darned endearing it made her sigh.

Tucking a stray lock of hair behind her ear, Seb sent shivery sensations the length of her body. "Good night, Counselor," he said, touching her elbow and gently guiding her to a position behind the wheel of her car.

Though he paid her lips homage with a lingering look beneath the starlit sky, Seb did not make a move to physically compromise Susan's determination to remain professionally detached from her client.

"Good night," she stammered in return, hoping it was too dark for him to see the disappointment shimmering in her eyes.

He shut the car door behind her and stepped aside.

Fumbling for the key she had left in the ignition, Susan prayed that the car, unlike her fickle heart, which had already stalled, would not fail her now. Not when she was so desperate to make a quick getaway.

Three

Susan awoke with a queasy feeling in the pit of her stomach. She had foolishly tucked herself into bed the night before, believing that everything would make sense in the morning. After hitting the snooze button on her alarm clock for the third consecutive time, she acknowledged that the jury was still out on what kind of traitorous tricks her body was playing on her. Suffice it to say, she hadn't slept well. A silver-eyed wolf haunted her dreams and kept her tossing in bed most of the night.

"Okay, Counselor," she said, recalling how the sound of that same impartial word rolling off her client's tongue had turned her bones to gelatin. "Time to get up and get a grip on yourself."

Dragging herself from the bed to the bathroom, Susan surveyed her disheveled image in the mirror.

Last night, with nothing more than a simple look and his sincere interest in her as a person, Seb had made her feel as glamorous as a movie star. This morning the light of day and the mirror on the wall refused to support such outrageous flights of imagination.

"I'm afraid you are not the fairest in the land, my dear," she muttered, reaching for a toothbrush and attempting to wash the taste of regret from her mouth. She hated facing her reflection so early in the morning with anything less than minty-fresh breath.

As usual, her long curly hair was an unruly mess. She grabbed a brush and attacked her mane with womanly vengeance. Susan knew that she was no beauty queen, a point her ex-husband drove home whenever the opportunity arose to compare her to another more-striking woman. Not driven by false modesty to call herself ugly, she was inclined to describe herself as merely ordinary. Her eyes, neither true green nor gray nor brown, were not, in her opinion, particularly noteworthy, and this morning she saw the beginning of worry lines at the corners.

Who was she kidding? Marriage to Joe might well have made those tiny furrows qualify as worry lines, but to the rest of the world they were nothing more than wrinkles, plain and simple. Hastily she applied a light layer of mascara and blush, chastising herself for wasting even this much time on her appearance. Had the last beautician she'd entrusted her tresses to not left her looking so mannish, to use Joe's word, she might have taken the scissors to the thick mane herself.

Acknowledging her golden locks as her only concession to vanity, Susan reminded herself that Joe had found her attractive enough once upon a time. Only after they had been married and she had declared her intention to go to law school had he become so critical of her. Having been raised in a highly traditional family in which his mother catered to his father's every need, Joe had clearly felt threatened by Susan's independent spirit. She wished she had spoken up more for herself when they were married. If she had, she supposed it would have been easier for her to remove the poisoned barbs that seemed to have found a permanent home in her psyche.

Even now she imagined that Joe would have been quick to attribute Sebastian's gallantry last night to her lack of feminine appeal. The sound of his taunting laughter echoed through her mind.

"It's not true," she told the skeptical reflection staring unblinkingly back at her. "He was simply being a gentleman by respecting my request not to blur the lines between our professional and personal lives."

That said, Susan tried to rouse a more genuine feeling of gratitude for Seb for not kissing her. He had, of course, been right in keeping their relationship on a completely professional level. Professional was what she wanted, after all.

Wasn't it?

The most astonishing thing about her reaction to Seb, Susan decided, was that she'd had any reaction to him at all. She had felt dead inside for so long that her physical awareness of Sebastian as a man was nothing short of monumental. Her friends had been telling her that it was past time she started living again. She supposed they were right. Two years of celibacy should be enough to get over her reservations about men in general and relationships with one in particular.

Regardless of the fact that Seb's easy self-control only served to underscore her doubts about her own ability to attract such a fascinating man, Susan knew with certainty that it would have been a horrible mistake to have indulged in the feeling of those firm, masculine lips on hers. She suspected the real reason she was feeling so let down was more of a testament to Seb's lack of interest in her as a woman than to her own good sense. Need she remind herself that she could ill afford to risk losing this case when so much was riding on it?

She sternly reminded herself that falling in love was a matter of choice. Only teenagers and incurable romantics could possibly believe otherwise. Who but the most naive could buy into the notion that love was an irresistible feeling that happened to you when the mischievous Cupid zapped you with one of his arbitrary magic arrows?

Falling in love was no different from choosing the right shade of lipstick. Susan picked up her favorite color and applied an even, light layer to lips that, usually full and smiling, now had too grim a set for so early in the day. The lipstick was a soft pink called "Almost There."

Too much like her life to be a coincidence....

Could it be that the universe was sending her subliminal messages telling her to hang in there?

For the hundredth time, Susan wondered if she really had what it took to make it in the field of law.

Was she truly lacking the killer instinct that her adviser had told her was a prerequisite for successful trial lawyers? Was she merely fooling herself, as Joe had insisted? The worst thing about losing her last two cases was not so much the financial strain it had put on her firm, but rather the way it had shaken her faith in herself.

Fortunately she had far too much to do today to wallow in pity or indulge in self-doubts. Incredible as it seemed, Sebastian Wescott had given her the opportunity of a lifetime, and she wasn't about to let a bad case of runaway hormones screw it up. The man needed a lawyer who was one hundred percent behind him, and she needed to focus all her efforts on being that lawyer. Needing to believe in her client's innocence before she could throw herself completely into representing him, she was ready to start dispelling her lingering doubts. Having spent such a pleasant evening with Sebastian Wescott the night before and actually coming to like him as a person, she was anxious to put her own mind at ease regarding his character.

While she knew many lawyers had no compunction about putting criminals back on the street, Susan was not one of them. If she was going to represent Sebastian, she wanted to be certain in her own mind that he was not guilty of the crime of which he was accused. And that meant she was going to have to prove to herself that her client was innocent beyond a shadow of a doubt, although in court the burden of proof was on the prosecutor and her job was only to establish "reasonable doubt."

She might be an idealist, but Susan had to believe

her client guiltless. For while she was not utterly in love with her reflection in the mirror, so far she'd had no reason to be ashamed of it. And no matter how much money or fame was involved, she wasn't about to start compromising her values just to make a name for herself.

Breakfast consisted of a cup of coffee and an energy bar, consumed while she flipped through her trusty time-planner and cleared her schedule. By the time she finished jotting down notes to herself, Susan wondered whether the United Nations would have been able to complete the ''to do'' list she had compiled for herself. Not the least of the items was the one to make sure that the next time she took a chance on a relationship, it was with a man more malleable than either her ex-husband or the dangerously charismatic Sebastian Wescott. Someone safer.

Someone more like his half brother, Dorian.

Distracted and irritable, Seb hadn't been himself all day. Everyone from his secretary to the mail clerk to his business associates had commented on it— behind his back, of course. All except for Rosa, who never was one to beat around the bush. Exasperated with his foul mood when he surprised her by coming home for lunch, she shooed him out of her kitchen, suggesting in not-so-gentle tones that he simply put himself out of his misery by phoning the woman who had his ''boxers in such a knot.''

''If anyone but you had the audacity to speak to me that way...'' Seb growled, wondering how she could possibly know it was a woman that was on his mind.

Rosa didn't bother letting him finish the thought. "Nobody but me knows you like I do. How many people can say they nursed you through chicken pox or saw you take your first steps or watched you running through the house buck-naked?"

Holding up an arthritic hand to stop him from responding, she exclaimed, "Wait! I really don't want to know the answer to that."

Seb laughed at his housekeeper's modesty. Since she had practically raised him by herself all those years when his father was off gallivanting around the world with his latest paramour, he wanted to put Rosa's mind at ease.

"Not as many as you and half the state of Texas, in particular the gossipmongers who print the society pages, would like to believe," he assured her.

"That's too bad. That business you're so fond of is no wife to you. A man needs a strong-headed, strong-hearted woman in his bed to remind him what's really important in life—and to keep his bloodline going. Which reminds me, just when do you intend to start filling this big old empty mansion with sweet-tempered, dirty-faced *bambinos* who look just like you used to?" Rosa demanded.

"What is it with everyone wanting to get me married off?" Seb asked in exasperation.

He was thinking about the bet he'd made earlier with four other bachelor members of the Cattleman's Club. This year, the dubious honor of heading up their annual Charity Ball fell to him. In a discussion with his friends over drinks, he had suggested that the last bachelor left standing among them by the time the ball itself rolled around would enjoy a "consolation'' party. At that time the lucky fellow would get to choose the charity to which all proceeds of the gala event would go. The bet had seemed harmless enough at the time, but in light of the investigation that had cast a pall over Seb's life, their lighthearted wager suddenly took on dark overtones. Chances were, the last bachelor would be left standing in prison.

It wasn't exactly the way Seb wanted to win a bet.

"Don't you think it might be wise to clear my name of murder charges before I start planning a family?" Seb asked with more concern than the devil-may-care smile on his face would have led Rosa to believe.

She clucked her tongue in censure of such an outlandish thought. "Don't you worry. Anyone who knows you at all knows that you're incapable of hurting another living creature. This little misunderstanding will be cleared up soon enough."

Not wanting to cause her undue anxiety, Seb didn't contradict her. There was no point in quibbling over words when the difference between a "misunderstanding" and a "murder" was the life of one of his business associates. Finding the scumbag who did Eric in was more important to Seb than simply clearing his own name. Vengeance might be the Lord's, but Seb wanted Eric Chambers's killer behind bars for the rest of his natural life. Whatever the outcome of the grand jury's investigation might be, Seb felt personally obligated to see that justice was done.

Grabbing the corned-beef-on-rye with hot mustard that Rosa offered him, he headed back to work with renewed resolve to set matters straight. The first thing he intended to do was call Robert Cole and see if any new leads had turned up. Having been led to believe that Cole was the best private investigator in the business, Seb was growing impatient with the lack of progress the detective was making.

When the true identity of the murderer eventually surfaced, Seb—who had devoted much of his adult life to protecting innocents in a world disinclined to defend the defenseless—was not above taking justice into his own hands. As a member of the Texas Cattleman's Club, he swore an oath to do no less.

Not that he would ever stoop to murder, however.

The next item on his agenda was to set up a meeting with Wescott Oil's legal team. Word around town was that Susan Wysocki's practice was all but washed up. However, he'd seen too much fire in those beautiful eyes of hers to believe that line of drivel. It never failed to amaze him how eager some members in the legal profession were to devour one another like piranhas. Hardly comforting to one in need of legal services. Nonetheless, while Seb was personally impressed with his lovely lawyer, he wasn't going to trust gut instinct alone. Not when he had such a wealth of resources at his fingertips to back her up if need be.

As long as Susan didn't think he was questioning her abilities, Seb didn't see what harm could come of bringing in some reinforcements. And if she didn't know anything about it, he didn't see how she could possibly object.

As luck would have it, Seb didn't have to make another appointment to see the woman who had been occupying so much of his thoughts. When he arrived at the Wescott office building, Susan was waiting outside for him, wearing a pensive look that stirred his protective instincts, and a fragrance that stimulated all his senses.

"What's wrong?" he asked, fighting the instinct to wrap his arms around her. To assure her that everything was going to work out just fine.

Her eyes shone with concern as she wrestled to find the best way to break the news to him. In the end she simply blurted it out.

"New evidence has come to light. From inside Wescott Oil, I'm afraid..."

Four

The Wescott building cast a long dark shadow over its namesake, a man currently wearing a grim expression as he leaned in to hear what the pretty woman standing next to him had to say. Even the most disinterested observer could discern that Sebastian Wescott was engaged in a very serious conversation. Only the most foolhardy would dare to interrupt such an exchange.

Or the most naive.

The little girl who approached the couple with tears in her eyes clearly fit into the latter category. So involved was Seb in the discourse that it took a tug on his shirtsleeve to get his attention. The glower on his face disappeared as soon as he realized that the interloper was no more than five or six years old. Matching red braids were slung haphazardly over a pair of narrow shoulders that shook with every sob the poor child took. Her plaid uniform identified her as a parochial-school student. More than likely an escapee from nearby St. Matthew's, Seb surmised, bending down to address her at eye level.

"What's the matter, sweetheart?" he asked.

"Mister, have you seen my mommy anywhere?" the girl asked.

Momentarily distracted from the impending legal crisis her client was facing, Susan joined the two of them in an uncomfortable—and what she was sure was an unladylike—squat on the sidewalk. Her skirt rode immodestly up on her thighs.

"You've lost your mother?" she asked, wiping away the child's tears with a decorative hankie she took from the breast pocket of her suit jacket. A light twill the color of daffodils, it was her favorite.

The girl took the silk cloth Susan offered and blew her nose into it. Hard and long.

"Uh-huh. She came to school with me today and talked to my class. It's Mother-Daughter Day, but mine forgot to take me with her to work like some of the other mothers did. So after recess I decided to come on my own."

A smile twitched at the corners of Seb's mouth when the little girl offered Susan back her hankie, soiled and soggy.

"Why don't you keep it in case you need it later?" Susan suggested. Folding the child's tiny hand over the swatch of cloth, she seemed in no hurry to let go. "What's your name, dear?"

"Carlie," replied the freckle-faced urchin. "Carlie Bachman. This is the building where my mommy works. She's a bookkeeper here. Some days she says it's a lot like being a zookeeper.''

"Is that right?'' Seb asked, unable to keep a note of amusement from creeping into his voice.

"Uh-huh,'' the child affirmed, turning her big green eyes skyward, as if by some act of magic these strangers would be able to pinpoint her mother's office hidden in the midst of the impressive eleven-story building. Glass dominated metal in its construction in much the same way the structure itself overshadowed the usually sleepy town of Royal. For a lost child, it might as well have been the giant beanstalk that Jack had grown from magic beans. Climbing it certainly seemed more daunting up close than it had seemed from the distance and safety of her classroom. A fresh batch of tears welled up in Carlie's eyes at the very prospect.

"Cheer up, darlin'. I have a sneaky suspicion that we can just go right on inside and rustle up your mom for you,'' Seb said with a reassuring smile. "What do you say we go find her right now?''

A look of relief crossed the girl's face as she threw her arms around Seb's neck and dried her tears on his collar. Not one for wasting any more time, she commanded in a tiny general's voice, "Let's go.''

Susan's heart lurched at the sight of Seb picking the child up in his arms as if it was the most natural thing in the world for him.

"Do you know my mommy?'' Carlie inquired of her hospitable mount.

"I sure do. In fact, I bet you've heard her refer to me as the head gorilla in this particular zoo,'' he explained with a straight face.

Seb did not stop at the front security desk to turn his ward over to someone else, as Susan had anticipated him doing. Rather, he strode right past, issuing a cordial "Hello, Jenkins," to the fellow on duty.

"Would you mind ringing Marilyn's office and telling her that I'm on my way up with a package for her from the lost-and-found department?"

"Yes, sir," Jenkins replied.

The smile the older man gave his boss seemed neither forced nor out of the ordinary. Susan was taken aback. Having initially figured Sebastian Wescott for the stereotypical cold corporate boss, she hadn't expected him to be on a friendly basis with his employees, let alone take such a personal interest in their lives. That he had put his own life crisis on hold to help this darling little girl locate her mother deepened her budding respect for him.

Like Seb, Joe had been both charismatic and highly resourceful. Resourceful enough to avoid paying his legal share of taxes and trimming employee benefits wherever he could, in fact. One thing her ex-husband lacked, however, that Seb seemed to have in abundance, was an innate sense of kindness. Just as his marvelous sense of humor lacked Joe's sarcastic edge, Seb's concern for others clearly was not based on his mood at the moment or on whether it advanced him personally.

"Mommy!"

The expression of joy that lit up Marilyn's face at the sight of her daughter in her boss's arms was swiftly followed by horror at the discovery of what her streetwise child had undertaken on her own.

"I've got to call the school and tell them where

you are, honey," she exclaimed, clearly thinking of Carlie's poor teacher combing the school looking for a truant kindergartner. "It will only take me a few minutes to drop her back off to school, if you don't mind, Mr. Wescott. I'd be glad to make up the time after hours," she offered apologetically.

Sebastian shrugged off the suggestion as if somehow offended by it. "I understand that today is Mother-Daughter Day. Since she seems to have her heart set on it, why don't you just let Carlie follow you around the job for a while, then knock off early for the rest of the day? Maybe you could take her to the zoo and show her the difference between the two places." He cleared his throat. "That is, if you can find any."

Though Marilyn colored deeply at the comment, it was not because Seb's teasing was in any way mean-spirited. In fact, everyone in the office within earshot roared as Carlie ventured an explanation.

"Little pictures have big ears, you know."

"Pitchers, dear, pitchers," her mother corrected.

The comment had more far-reaching ramifications for Wescott Oil than appeared at first blush, Susan mused. For just as little Carlie had accidentally "leaked" information from her mother to her employer, Susan had the unpleasant task of explaining to Seb that someone in his company was leaking damaging information about him directly to the police.

Once mother and child were properly reunited and settled into their adjusted schedule for the day, Sebastian directed Susan to accompany him to the tower floor, where they could "continue their conversation privately.'' Rumor had it that the eleventh floor—also referred to as the executive floor—was reserved for Seb's office. A tasteful plaque on a door of polished brass and glass announced to visitors that they were entering the domain of Wescott Oil's CEO. Susan was duly impressed as she stepped into the walnut-paneled office.

Elegantly furnished, it was open and airy. An entire wall of windows provided a panoramic view of Royal and the surrounding countryside. As in the construction of his home, Seb had somehow managed to bring a rural, comfortable feel to his sophisticated surroundings. A solid oak door situated unostentatiously behind a fully stocked wet bar gave no clue to what lay beyond.

"That's my private suite,'' Seb explained, noticing her staring intently at the door, as if trying to penetrate it with X-ray vision. "It's just a place to conk out when the midnight oil runs low. I've been offered my father's old office, but I'm partial to this one.''

He didn't bother adding that the plush office suite was part of what Rosa blamed for his prolonged state of bachelorhood. "When a man makes a habit of sleeping with his business, what need has he of a wife?'' she'd lamented on more than one occasion.

Susan was too polite to inquire further. As much as she would have liked to satisfy her curiosity with a personal tour, it was enough to know that her client was no mere figurehead in the business his father had begun. That he explained his suite as a means of enabling him to work longer hours, rather than as the playboy's love nest that rumor alleged it, was oddly comforting. Susan told herself that was only because representing a jaded playboy was much less palatable than representing an overly dedicated CEO—it was surely not that she had any personal interest in Sebastian Wescott.

Still, the very thought of a bedroom strategically located behind this door was enough to rattle any woman's composure. An image of Seb stretched out on a king-size bed wrapped in nothing but a silk sheet made her mouth grow dry and her palms sweaty.

"Are you sure it's safe to talk in here?" she asked abruptly, hoping to focus her wayward thoughts in a more appropriate direction.

Seb looked startled by the question. "Do you have any reason to believe otherwise?" he wanted to know.

Susan offered up the facts without bothering to sugarcoat them.

"You mean, aside from the damaging e-mail with your name attached that was supposedly sent from here? The one so easily intercepted by the police? The one incriminating you in the murder of Eric Chambers?" she asked, arms akimbo. "Or maybe the discovery of substantial funds in a private account established in your name? Evidence, need I remind you, that was also discovered in this very office."

The man standing before her was suddenly transformed into a vision of a fierce modern-day warrior. Anger bunched the muscles beneath his shirt, balled his hands into fists and clenched his jaw. And those silver wolflike eyes narrowed into wounded slits of rage.

Susan braced herself. Wanting to see how her client would react under pressure on the stand, she had deliberately goaded him. She had fully expected him to behave in a manner similar to Joe's whenever someone called his controversial business practices into question. Invariably, Joe would adopt a threatening posture and launch into a defensive tirade, casting blame on everyone else, designed to make the person who had questioned his integrity eventually feel guilty for having done so.

But contrary to her expectations, Seb turned icy in his fury. The glance he turned on her could have frozen the water in the crystal pitcher on the table next to her. Susan fought the urge to rub the goose bumps from her bare arms.

"Do you mean to say that you suddenly find my case hopeless, or that you've simply decided I'm guilty as charged and would like to be relieved of the responsibility of defending me?" Seb asked her.

Susan knew it was risky to continue pushing a man when he was so clearly outraged by her frontal attack upon his good name. But the risk had to be taken. Whether or not it cost her this case, it was imperative for Susan to gauge Seb's reaction to her line of questioning. As frightening as the prospect was to her, catching him off guard was crucial to her strategy.

"How do you feel about having a traitor in your midst, Seb? Tell me, is there anyone in this entire building you can trust?"

Eyes the color of quicksilver captured her gaze and held it.

"You," he answered without hesitation.

Susan felt her pulse quicken. For a man who was

generally considered to be cool and calculating in business, Seb seemed to her far too trusting for his own good. Certainly he didn't know her well enough to be putting such faith in her ability to clear his name. Especially when this case became more complicated with every question she asked. Was it any wonder someone had infiltrated the ranks of Wescott Oil? For all Seb knew, the charming bookkeeper he had just granted the afternoon off might be plotting to do him harm. Who knew what drove an employee to stab his employer in the back? Not to mention the enemies Sebastian might have in rival competitors in the industry.

They couldn't afford to disregard any potential suspects. But it certainly wouldn't be easy enlisting Seb's help in flushing them out. Seemingly disgruntled employees were unheard of here. After all, Sebastian Wescott was generally liked and respected in the community. Active in the Texas Cattleman's Club, he was well-known for his generosity in contributing to needy charities. Moreover, a job at Wescott Oil was coveted in the town of Royal. Seb didn't seem to begrudge paying his employees wages well above the average for the area. In addition, he offered one of the best benefit packages around. And having witnessed the easy camaraderie he displayed with his employees, Susan suspected he would be deeply hurt if any one of them was unmasked as a Judas.

The hurt written on his features was unmistakable, but it wasn't new, Susan realized with a start.

"You already knew about the mole in your operation, didn't you?" she asked, reading his body language correctly.

"It isn't hard putting two and two together," he said, sinking wearily into his leather desk chair. "My compliments to you on coming to the same conclusion I did far quicker than the local police. I understand that they all but have me convicted down at the local doughnut shop."

His attempt at humor was halfhearted, but his respect for Susan's astuteness was genuine. That she had pieced together crucial information in an incredibly short amount of time and made a leap of faith was nothing short of astonishing. And her refusal to take all those bits of incriminating evidence and convict him in her own heart—or to look for some technical loophole to get him off rather than accept his claim of innocence—did more than simply endear her to him. It made him believe without a doubt that she was the right person to represent him.

"I am in my brother's debt," he said, meaning it.

Susan accepted the compliment with a hesitant smile. Wishing she could help ease his worries, she fought the urge to slip behind him and knead the knotted muscles in his shoulders. It surprised her to think that the crisis in their tenuous relationship had passed over as quickly as storm clouds blowing across a Texas sky in April.

"Did I hear my name taken in vain?" asked a disembodied voice preceding its owner into the room.

Susan was startled to see Dorian standing in the doorway as if waiting for permission to enter. She thought she remembered Sebastian closing the door behind them earlier, and wondered just how long Dorian had been privy to their conversation. Dressed in a dark turtleneck and slacks, he was the picture of studied casualness.

"Just thought I'd drop by and ask if you two would like to go to dinner with me," he said, giving the impression that he had just now stumbled upon the two of them.

Susan tried resurrecting an interest in Dorian rather than his brother as he stepped into the room. Unfortunately, with the two of them standing side by side there was no use denying that Seb overpowered Dorian in every way. A wannabe clone of his half brother, Dorian lacked not only Seb's imposing physical presence but also his can-do, don't-even-think-about-getting-in-my-way aura of assuredness that was so very compelling in the business world. Dorian might have a smoother, less-formidable exterior, but Susan wondered if he would have bothered taking the time to personally escort a lost child back to her mother.

Feeling guilty about comparing the two brothers, she forced a smile for the man who had brought them all together. She, too, owed him a debt of gratitude for recommending her to Seb in the first place. Assuming that there was at least one, if not more, saboteurs employed by Wescott Oil, Seb would need all the support she could muster. That Dorian had access not only to workers' computer files but also to their inner sanctum—the employee lounge—was a tremendous advantage. An employee himself, he had limited anonymity in not sharing his father and brother's infamous last name.

"I don't suppose you've heard anything unusual from the other employees in the building that might be helpful to your brother's case, have you?'' Susan asked him.

The question appeared to catch him off guard. He stammered uncomfortably before admitting to Seb that "just about everyone seems worried about losing their jobs if you're found guilty.''

"Their loyalty is touching,'' Seb muttered dryly.

Although Dorian's statement provided neither comfort nor insight into the case, Susan was not about to be dissuaded from her cause. She continued thinking aloud.

"Who has access to this office?'' she wanted to know. As far as she was concerned, Dorian's own ability to simply waltz in unannounced didn't speak well of security measures.

"Do you know of any disgruntled employees who might want their boss behind bars? Anyone you can think of who would enjoy playing the part of a corporate mole?'' she persisted.

That Dorian didn't look surprised at the very suggestion of such treachery was an ominous sign in itself.

"If you're asking me if I've been keeping my ear to the ground, of course I have,'' he replied smoothly. A sympathetic expression on his features, he turned his attention to his brother. "I hate to be the one to break it to you, big brother, but it's not going to be so easy narrowing down all the people who aren't particularly thrilled with your management style.''

For a suave businessman who was reputed to dine among the sharks, Sebastian Wescott didn't hide his feelings very well. He looked surprised. And very, very hurt.

Susan could understand his reaction. From everything she had heard and personally witnessed, Sebastian Wescott was an exemplary boss. Of course, one could never discount the resentment of an employee who had been let go for one reason or another. Also there was the general sense of bitterness so many people harbored toward the wealthy, targeting them as objects of hatred for no other reason than their success—regardless of whether they had come by their fortune honestly or not, and regardless of whether they spent it altruistically or selfishly.

Susan suspected the prosecution would do everything in its power to capitalize on such irrational beliefs and attempt to demonize Seb as a robber baron of old. She wondered if the jury would take into account all the jobs and revenue Wescott Oil Enterprises provided for their hometown. Her heart twisted at the thought of how painful it would be for Seb to endure denunciations from any employees willing to publicly bite the hand that fed them. Fortunately, having seen him in action earlier with Carlie, she didn't think it would be too hard coming up with loyal employees eager to attest to their employer's character.

"Can you get me a list of people who've been fired from Wescott Oil, starting with the most recent and working backward?" she asked Dorian. "Everyone from the janitor pool to the inner sanctum of top management."

"How soon do you need it?"

Her smile was weary as she responded, "Yesterday."

After assuring her that he would get her a computer printout as soon as possible, Dorian attempted to lighten the mood by reminding them of his offer to take them both out to dinner. Seb looked pleased by the opportunity to focus on happier times. Clearly the impending lawsuit was taking more of a toll on him than he'd like those closest to him to believe.

Susan could empathize. She had been working hard on this case, and she knew from experience that often the best insights came to her in relaxed settings where her brain wasn't on overload trying to unravel a complex case.

"What a lovely, generous offer," she said, bestowing on Dorian a look of gratitude. She knew his brother was going to need all the friends he could find in the difficult days ahead.

"Count me in," Seb chimed in. "Just so long as you let me pick up the tab. It's the least I can do to thank you for finding me such a crackerjack lawyer."

Dorian protested, but not very hard, Susan noticed. He did, however, look visibly moved by Seb's next remark as he offered his brother his hand in a time-honored and sacred gesture.

"You have no idea how much your support means to me, Dorian. I'm proud to call you my brother."

Suddenly feeling like an intruder, Susan tried swallowing the lump that rose in her throat. Yet witnessing the two men, so similar in physical appearance, clasping hands in the symbolic bond of brotherhood, she felt a sense of dire foreboding for which there was simply no explanation.

Five

___

As the evening progressed, it became excruciatingly apparent that whatever her earlier premonition had been about, it had little to do with any rivalry between the two brothers over her. Dorian seemed completely uninterested in her as anything more than his brother's legal representation. She liked to think it was because he sensed his brother was attracted to her, but it seemed unlikely that a man as sought-after as Sebastian Wescott would be interested in a woman so clearly his socioeconomic inferior. In previous conversations she had alluded to feeling deprived as a child. Susan didn't think he understood that she was referring to more than the lack of a new bicycle any more than she could grasp the meaning of his cryptic comment about his own underprivileged youth.

After making a point of seating her beside Seb, Dorian sat in a chair across the table from them and proceeded to spend the rest of the evening fawning over every remark that came out of his brother's mouth. When he wasn't agreeing with what Seb said, he seemed to be raising doubts about every employee with whom he'd ever come in contact. Doggedly persistent, he ignored every attempt of Seb's to change the conversation. Susan visibly tensed when he approached the wine list as if it were a register of possible suspects.

Making an effort to relax, she gratefully allowed Seb to pour her another glass of wine. He looked debonair and handsome in a light-blue striped shirt and navy tie of fine imported silk. Seb was the real thing—he didn't have to adopt the pretensions of his less-assured brother.

Considering his background, she knew she was being too hard on Dorian. She supposed he was entitled to put on airs. In all likelihood it was just his way of dealing with old childhood insecurities. Glancing around the room, Susan could see why this restaurant drew such a wealthy clientele from miles around. Evidently word was out that the food at Claire's was as outstanding as its distinctly upscale atmosphere. Everything from the valet parking out front to the fine linen tablecloths to the fresh-cut roses at every table to the imported wines and gourmet French cuisine implied that status was for sale here.

Staring into the gentle flicker of candlelight, Susan wondered if Dorian would ever stop talking long enough for her to enjoy the soothing ambiance. She was actually relieved when his cell phone interrupted his incessant prattle and he excused himself to take the call in private. The ensuing silence was blissful.

When Seb reached across the table to take her hand in his, Susan felt a surge of warmth.

"He means well," Seb told her, acknowledging with the statement his own irritation with Dorian.

Susan found his loyalty touching.

"By the way, you look lovely tonight."

The compliment was more intoxicating than the expensive wine they were drinking. Normally Susan would be more wary of such glib flattery if it hadn't sounded so sincere. She brushed it aside uneasily.

"I mean it," Seb persisted. "You are a beautiful woman, and it concerns me that you seem so completely unaware of it. If things weren't so complicated, so crazy, in my life right now, I'd spend all of my time proving that to you."

Feeling transformed by the admiration glimmering in his eyes, Susan squeezed his hand and blinked back the moisture that clouded her vision. It was the sweetest thing anyone had ever said to her.

"Thank you," she said, meaning it. "You're not so bad on the eyes yourself."

That her ex-husband should choose that exact moment to waltz into the restaurant seemed a cruel trick of fate. All her pretty illusions shattered like a mirrored ball crashing to the floor of some make-believe cotillion. Susan wished that she could slip unnoticed beneath the table.

Though it came as no surprise to Susan that Joe had some cute young thing hanging on his arm, she was not at all prepared for the gut-wrenching impact of their entrance on her. The baby-faced nymphet with Joe had a body made for spandex, and knowing Joe's preferences, Susan assumed she had a shrink-wrapped brain, as well. Judging by the satisfied expression he wore, Susan knew it was too much to hope that her ex would simply pass by their table with a perfunctory hello.

"Well," he drawled, stopping and sizing her up from top to bottom as if perusing an old, familiar novel. One with tattered and dog-eared pages.

Feeling obligated to introduce him to Seb and Dorian, who had just returned to the table, Susan put on a tight smile. "Gentlemen, my ex-husband, Joe Wysocki."

Before she could present him with their names, however, Joe gave her a condescending smirk and said, "Business must be better than rumor has it if you can still afford to dine at Claire's."

His insult carried the force of a slap in the face. Not wanting to give him the satisfaction of knowing how easily he still got to her, she willed aside the moisture clouding her vision. What was it about this man that took her back in time to the tender vulnerabilities of her youth? A youth when she was besotted with the idea of marrying an older, more sophisticated man. The cruel intent with which Joe attempted to undermine her confidence tonight was nothing new, but Susan found herself unable to think of a witty rejoinder to take the sting out of his insult. To her surprise—and, she secretly acknowledged, pleasure—Susan was momentarily taken aback when Seb took it upon himself to defend her.

Eyes the color of smoking gunmetal impaled Joe. "I'm not in the habit of asking a lady to pay for her own meal when she's in my company. If that's a problem for you, I'd suggest your daughter join our party for the remainder of the evening.''

A man more comfortable hurling slurs than enduring them, Joe turned crimson with anger as Susan fought back the laughter tickling the back of her throat. It was a relief to discover that she wasn't the only one who thought Joe looked ridiculous with this pubescent arm candy attached to him. Almost ten years older than Susan, Joe was indeed old enough to be this young woman's father.

"Tamara is not my daughter," he said, slipping an arm possessively around her tiny waist. "She happens to be my date."

"How embarrassing—for you," Seb murmured without an ounce of remorse. "Next time you swing by the high school, be sure to tell all your friends that business has picked up for Susan. Apparently they're unaware that she's been hired to represent Sebastian Wescott in the highest-profile case this dusty little town will likely see for quite some time."

With that, he turned his attention back to Susan, effectively snubbing Joe, who stood beside their table picking up his jaw from the top of his expensive Italian shoes.

"And under whose authority have you come by this piece of information?" Joe sputtered in disbelief.

That he seemed more intent upon finding out the status of his ex-wife's business rather in than taking umbrage at the slight on his companion's age didn't appear to sit any better with young Tamara than with Susan herself. Remembering a time when she had attributed such disrespect to the difference in their ages and Joe's brash business style, Susan pitied the younger woman. If she hoped to obtain the security of Joe's money, Tamara would, Susan knew, be forced to give up her identity in order to meet Joe's every need. She wished there was some way to warn Joe's next intended victim that the money was not worth it.

"None other than the client himself," Seb replied. "Now, if you don't mind, I'd like to get back to a grown-up conversation with my lawyer. I'm sure the maître d' will bring your date a Shirley Temple while you wait at the bar for your own table. As you can see, this one is already taken."

As was every other table in the room. Leave it to Joe to show up without a reservation and expect to be seated right away. Furthermore his pushy, condescending attitude did little to endear him to the serving staff, who disdainfully informed him he'd have to wait his turn. Among the influential clientele of Claire's, some of whom had flown in from out of state, Joe Wysocki pulled little weight. Susan was delighted to see him forced to choose between making a scene and slinking to the bar in compliance with Seb's directive.

Not at all inclined to get himself barred from the most exclusive restaurant in town, Joe tossed a final insult over his shoulder as he guided Tamara in the direction of the bar in the adjoining room. "You'd think a millionaire would have more sense than to hire some second-rate lawyer to defend him."

"You'd think any man but a consummate jackass would know better than to let a woman as beautiful and amazing as Susan get away,'' Seb rejoined, loud enough for everyone in the establishment to hear.

By no means a small man, Joe was used to intimidating others with his size and demeanor. He wheeled around, his hands balled into fists at his sides. But the challenge on his lips died as Seb rose to his feet. He stood several inches taller than Joe, and the steely look in his eyes left no doubt that he was not one to back down from a fight. The moment seemed like an eternity to Susan, who remembered to breathe only after Joe finally yielded to his opponent's clearly superior physical powers and simply opted to leave.

Like the Cheshire cat, all that remained of him was a nasty sneer hanging in the air—or rather imprinted on Susan's mind. Though she had done her best to remain perfectly calm during the heated exchange, her hands were shaking when she picked up her wineglass and lifted it to her lips.

''I can't believe you were ever married to such an arrogant little...''

Unable to think of a socially appropriate word, Seb let the unfinished sentence hang in the air.

''Me, neither.''

Blushing the color of the wine in her glass, Susan smiled at him gratefully. Had it been anyone but Joe, she would not have been so lost for words. As much as she hated for Seb to think her incapable of standing up for herself, it had certainly been gallant of him to defend her honor. From the horrified expression still lingering on Dorian's face, she would have been waiting a long time indeed for *him* to speak up on her behalf. Susan wondered if she should offer to perform the Heimlich maneuver on him to reestablish his normal breathing pattern.

"I'd like to call it an evening," Dorian said.

"That sounds like a good idea," Susan seconded, eager to put as much distance between herself and her ex as possible. One never knew what Joe might do once he had a couple of drinks in him. And she'd had quite enough of his behavior for one lifetime.

When Seb offered to drive her home, she gratefully accepted. Two glasses of wine was her limit, and she had no desire to explain herself to a police officer had she the misfortune to be pulled over. Besides, she wasn't ready to part company with Seb just yet. Every minute she spent with him brought new insight into what this man was really made of. He was what her father liked to refer to as a "real man's man." Charm, strength, intelligence and integrity all wrapped up in one appealing physical package, Sebastian Wescott appeared to be a true gentleman through and through. He wasn't at all the snobbish exemplar of the ultrarich she had once envisioned. This was definitely a man worth getting to know better. A man who deserved to have his day in court represented by someone who genuinely cared about him.

Susan noticed the surprised look on Seb's face when she asked him if he'd like to come up to her apartment a short while later. She was glad when he agreed to walk her to the door. That her actions seemed less than professional was of little consequence at the moment. Feeling particularly melancholy about the events of the evening, she didn't want to be alone with nothing better to do than brood over Joe's verbal abuse. All she had to do was see her ex, and she was back on the same emotional roller coaster she had ridden for the duration of her marriage.

It wasn't until Seb stepped inside her apartment that she became self-conscious, thinking how different it was from his luxurious estate. Except for the papers scattered from one end to the other, indicating her dedication to his case, little about her home reflected her own personality. In her divorce, Susan had been more than willing to give Joe the showplace of a house he had insisted they buy, and all the luxurious contents he had acquired by maxing out their credit cards.

Looking around her modest surroundings through Seb's eyes, she supposed her life looked empty and pathetic to him. Despite the fact that she paid a handsome price every month to secure her lease on this place, it did look rather like a college dorm—minus the posters on the walls. In truth, this apartment was simply a temporary place to sleep and eat until the future chose to reveal itself to her. The only photograph on display was of her family, and it was sorely dated.

"I want to thank you properly," she told Seb, moving a stack of documents to clear a place for him on her sofa. A cheerful slipcover hid the fact that the fabric of the rented furniture was worn through on the armrests.

"For what?" he asked.

That he looked genuinely perplexed by her words only served to deepen the sense of gratitude Susan felt. She sat down beside him, slipped her shoes off her aching feet and looked him directly in the eyes. Falling helplessly into their silvery depths, she spied compassion—and something more....

"For standing up to Joe back there, of course," she said in a throaty, emotional voice that she hardly recognized as hers. "For such a very public show of support."

Seb put his index finger beneath her chin and tilted up her head so she couldn't avoid the heat of his gaze. "That was nothing compared to what I'd like to do for you."

Susan went all soft and warm inside at the images his words conjured up. Her breath came in shallow, feathery gasps, and her pulse skittered in a most alarming pattern. Recognizing that her reaction was far from professional did absolutely nothing to change the fact that she wanted to feel Seb's lips on hers more than she had ever wanted anything in her life. To see for herself if there were more than empty promises smoldering behind those intriguing dark lashes of his. She longed for one brief, stolen moment to indulge her senses and feel like a hot-blooded woman, instead of a cool, logical lawyer.

Recalling the last time her eyelids had drifted shut in expectation of a kiss—and the disappointment that followed when Seb had so chivalrously refused to take advantage of her momentary weakness—she tried to tear her gaze away from the sensuous curve of his lips. And failed miserably. It was as if her brain, overloaded with worries and overwhelmed by the latest encounter with her ex-husband, had simply shut down and given her body complete authority to override her tenuous willpower.

"We both know what a bad idea this is," Susan murmured in a last-ditch attempt to resuscitate reason.

She wondered if Seb was as confused by the contradiction in her words and actions as she was herself. Curling her legs beneath her, she proceeded to wrap her arms around his neck. She was glad that he didn't attempt to remove them. Rather, she felt a shudder run through him and saw the impact of her touch reflected in the shimmering depths of the identical wells that were his eyes. Thus emboldened, she lifted her face to his and pressed her lips against temptation. To her delight, she found everything she'd secretly hoped for, as Seb responded with an ardor that set the earth trembling beneath them both.

Never had she thought a simple kiss could have such an impact on all her senses at once.

It was akin to diving off a precipice and embracing the fall. All thoughts of the abrupt stop at the bottom vanished in the exquisite joy of the moment. There was no denying that she wanted him. Not when the whimper that rose in her throat belied all rational thought and gave away her emotions in kittenish tones.

Or was it a wildcat that Seb had released from its bonds with his oh-so-tender kisses? Her lips parted, inviting a deeper sharing of the intimacy crackling between them like bolts of lightning illuminating the night sky. Susan melted against him. He proceeded in a slow, cautious manner, as if careful not to frighten her or cause her to draw away. Seb was an expert kisser—she had to give him that—and he evoked in her a passion that thrilled her like nothing in her previous experience. She felt as powerful as a lion tamer.

And as beautiful as a butterfly spreading its wings for the first time since escaping its cocoon.

Gone was the sense of deep inadequacy she had always felt with Joe. In place of the awkward girlish lover she considered herself to be was a woman secure in her own sensuality. In the loving circle of this man's arms, she did not shy away from the passion he offered, but rather opened herself up to it fully. She slipped her hands to his collar and unloosened his tie. The buttons of his shirt gave way beneath her eager fingertips.

When his hands reached up to stop her, Susan's newfound sense of feminine prowess splintered into shards of broken glass and pierced her vulnerable heart. Hot tears rose to her eyes and clouded her vision. It was no code of ethics governing lawyer-client relations that was stopping him from taking her on the spot as she so desperately wanted. No, she told herself, shattered. The fact that Seb pulled away from her advances could mean but one thing.

He simply didn't want her.

Six

Seb wanted this woman as he had never wanted any woman before. What he was feeling was more than mere physical longing. He cared for Susan, as well. From the very first time he'd laid eyes on her, she stirred a protective response in him that he had never felt for another. Many was the time he had played the part of the hero in carrying out covert missions for the Texas Cattleman's Club, but never had he felt such an overwhelming need as the need he felt now, to see himself reflected in this woman's eyes as someone worthy of her consideration. Unfortunately the fact that she was defending him against charges of murder made that an extraordinarily difficult task.

When her cocky little jerk of an ex-husband had gone out of his way to be rude back at Claire's, Seb found it hard confining himself to verbal jabs alone.

What he'd really wanted to do was break a few more blood vessels in that bulbous drinker's nose of Joe's by driving a fist through his smug expression. If Joe Wysocki was that vicious in public, Seb wondered how he had treated Susan in private. The thought of her enduring that kind of abuse caused the blood to bubble and surge through his body in angry spurts.

Having seen the pain reflected in Susan's big, doe-like eyes and witnessed firsthand how she curled protectively around herself like a seashell in the man's presence, Seb did not want to take advantage of her simply because she was feeling vulnerable tonight. Still, if their relationship was to move to the next level, he planned to offer this woman more than a shoulder to cry on. He needed to be wanted with the same intensity that he felt for her. Though Seb considered himself a good man, he had no desire to be a saint.

He wasn't exactly sure what he was feeling…beyond overpowering desire. He only knew that when he had first posed that ridiculous bet down at the Texas Cattleman's Club about who would be the last bachelor standing at their annual charity ball, he had never dreamed such a phenomenal woman would enter his life—and certainly not under such bizarre circumstances. In light of the fact that he might well be spending the night of the big charity ball doing time rather than orchestrating the social event of the year, it hardly seemed fair to ask Susan to consider him a potential suitor.

Indeed, the possibility of marriage had crossed his devoted housekeeper's mind far more often than it did his own. For as many years as Rosa had been after him to find a nice woman and settle down, she had never been particularly impressed with the predatory women who had set their sights on him. She sized them up truthfully enough: pretty, flighty things able to carry on little conversation beyond the gossip presented in the local society pages and incapable of calculating beyond the impact that his considerable fortune would have on their lives. On the whole, Seb considered them too much like the young gold diggers his father fancied to be taken very seriously. Susan's humble background, altruism and sense of independence made her completely different from other women who had slipped in and out of his life like ghosts. He felt certain that Rosa would approve of her.

That is, if he could stop Susan from running out on him right here and now. She jumped up from the couch with unshed tears glistening in her eyes and glanced at her watch.

"It's late. You'd better get on home."

Seb reached out and gently encircled her wrist with one hand.

"I think you misunderstood my intentions. I certainly didn't mean to insult you," he said softly, drawing her back into his lap and letting her know just how aroused she made him. "I want to be sure that you don't feel pressured to do anything that you'll regret later. I don't want to be held solely responsible for crossing that precious lawyer-client boundary that you've been using as a shield to keep me at arm's distance since the first time I expressed an interest in you as a woman."

Susan stopped tugging to be released from his grip

long enough to consider his feelings. He was right, of course. She wasn't being fair to him—or to herself, for that matter.

"I shouldn't have to remind you that I'm not your ex-husband," Seb chided softly. His gaze never wavered as he searched the depths of her soul through the mirrors of her eyes. "Or some jerk who wants nothing more than the bragging rights to a one-night stand. If you want me to stay the night, Susan, you'll have to be the one to do the asking. And you need to be prepared to have me stick around for more than breakfast the next morning."

Susan felt a fire building behind her eyes. It wasn't the kind of speech she expected to hear from a man whom the social pages characterized as a world-class womanizer. Truly, his words were as honest and forthright as the desire shining in his eyes. It was a refreshing change to be treated by a man as an equal rather than as a puppet to be manipulated and controlled.

Yielding to an impulse, she leaned forward and kissed Seb on the cheek. "That's for giving me the opportunity to make up my own mind," she told him, noting the disappointment that crossed Seb's features as he struggled to accept her apparent decision to keep their relationship on a strictly professional level.

"And this," she added, slipping her hands inside his shirt, "is for allowing me the prerogative of changing it."

Never had she felt so brazen or powerful as when her touch caused him to moan aloud. The sound of it reverberated through her body like a tuning fork, making it hum in eager expectation. Feeling a surge of womanly confidence, Susan didn't fumble with the buttons on his shirt as she had before, but rather freed them all with the expertise of one far more schooled in the art of seduction than she actually was. Her lips sought the sensitive hollow between his collarbones. From there she trailed kisses along the curve of his neck to his square jaw, where the stubble of a day's growth of beard brushed against her own tender flesh and thrilled her with its unmistakable masculinity.

Clothes littered the floor in a trice. A woman's yellow suit jacket, a silk tie, shoes, socks, all marked the path to a tidy little bedroom. Since she'd occupied this apartment, no man had lain on her new violet-patterned sheets. If the decor was too feminine for his tastes, Seb did not say so as he carried her to the bed, tore back the comforter and placed her upon those clean, inviting sheets. He paused a moment to gaze at her half-naked beauty as one would behold a painting of inestimable worth.

Slowly and with utmost care, he proceeded to finish undressing her. First the silken shirt that hung only where it was tucked into her skirt. He paused to pay her breasts tribute by cupping them in both hands and depositing kisses on their creamy abundance before unsnapping the fastener at the back of her satin-and-lace bra and feasting his eyes on all their loveliness.

At his pronouncement that they were "perfect," Susan felt relief wash over her. Pleased that she hadn't disappointed him, she lifted her hips off the mattress to assist in the act of divesting herself of her matching split skirt and nylons. By the time Seb reached for her lacy panties, Susan thought she was going to die from pleasure. It was so sublime that every cell in her body throbbed in anticipation. That his body was reacting in a similar fashion was undeniable and incredibly gratifying to a woman who up until this very moment had been uncertain about her ability to please a man sexually.

Erotic silhouettes danced against the walls in the light cast by a bulb burning in the hallway. Time slowed as minute details became succulent morsels of sensuality to savor. Seeing Seb undress was less an act of voyeurism than the beholding of something awesome. Susan watched in reverence.

Standing well over six feet, he looked to her like a beautiful warrior worthy of comparison to a Michelangelo sculpture. Seb was quick, however, to remind her that he was not made of stone but of flesh. He reached out and took one of her feet into his hands and began kneading it softly. The act brought tears to Susan's eyes. Never before had she been treated to such tender foreplay. Never had she been pleasured so skillfully.

In Seb's hands, she felt herself a sacred object.

From the soles of her feet, he massaged his way along her ankles to her calves, pausing to nibble whenever he felt the need. By the time he reached her thighs, Susan was moaning. Unaware of the sounds emanating from someplace faraway and deep inside, she was conscious only of the feel of flesh against flesh, of lips devouring her and making her whole. She opened her heart to him, silently begging him to stop, hoping he would not.

''Not yet,'' he said. His voice was the sound of

water washing gravel down a stream and had the power to smooth rough edges from the sharpest pebbles.

Susan wondered what she would do if the dam restraining Seb's passion broke and the floodwaters swept her away to places she had never been. Would she revel in it, emerging anew, like Aphrodite from the foam?

Seb did not give her the opportunity to consider such matters long. Kissing the feminine curve of her tummy, he dispersed such thoughts along with any haunting reminders of how Joe had enjoyed finding fault with the body singing beneath a gentler man's touch. Susan cried out as he suckled her breasts, worshiping each equally and reiterating his opinion that she was flawless.

He kissed her so thoroughly that Susan yearned for consummation as never before. She beseeched him with more than her eyes alone to take her completely. That he was able to remember protection at such a time surprised her—she herself was beyond rational thought. Though she knew she would appreciate his wisdom later, right now she wanted to know that this brief hiatus taxed him, as well as her. Needing proof of the power she exercised over him, she took Seb intimately into her hands and was gratified to find him rock hard.

"See what you do to me?" he murmured, demanding that she take ownership of the state of his arousal.

Lowering himself to her, he murmured her name as if uttering a prayer.

Simultaneously Susan cried out Seb's name in

astonishment. Having had but one lover before him, she was not prepared to be filled so completely or to succumb so fully to a manliness that demanded so much of her body without intentionally inflicting pain. Indeed, Seb had no need of trying to make himself seem bigger than he actually was in any way whatsoever.

On the verge of losing control, he somehow managed to restrain himself. "Am I hurting you?" he asked, searching her eyes in the dim light for the truth, for fear she might well lie just to spare his feelings.

Not yet, she longed to tell him, suspecting the real hurt would come later, after the sweet soreness of the lovemaking had long faded. She wasn't sure whether her poor heart could survive the memory of a night such as this, could not bear the thought of going back to the lonely life that had been hers before Seb had made her his own.

Not to be dissuaded by logic, her body refused to allow her mind to override passion. Flesh demanded no more than what the moment had to offer, and it had far, far more to offer than Susan had ever thought possible between a man and a woman. Slick with wanting, her tender flesh stretched to accept a union in which two became one.

Bodies throbbing with tension seemed to share the same breath as they scaled heights few dared to attempt. Reaching the peak was exquisite torture, as each movement brought them closer and closer to a sweet release that promised to open the doors of bliss. Glistening with sweat, they clung to one another and rode out the explosion that rocked the earth beneath them and metaphorically aligned the stars blinking in the heavens above. Together they drifted away to an emotional plane where souls achieved the freedom of weightlessness.

Left behind, their bodies trembled in aftershock, and they took pleasure in slowly subsiding pulsation.

"Hold me through the night," Susan entreated, fearing that if she closed her eyes, Seb would disappear, leaving her to curse a dream too sweet to be true. She clung to him.

Along with a strand of hair that had fallen haphazardly across her cheek, he brushed away her insecurities. Arranging her hair on the pillow so that it resembled a halo, he assured her, "I'm not going anywhere."

He hoped not, anyway, brushing away thoughts about the impending trial that could well rob him of his freedom. Clearly Susan was worried that the case was not going well.

Long past the time when her breathing deepened into sound and peaceful sleep, he lay awake studying her. Smart, funny, sexy—and clearly terrified of falling in love again—she was unlike anyone he had ever known before. Despite a difficult childhood and a monstrous marriage, she'd retained an innocence that touched something so deep inside him that he trembled as he placed a kiss on her cheek. Repose smoothed the worry lines from her face, making her look like an angel.

Seb felt a fierce surge of tenderness as he watched her sleep. Suddenly this devoted bachelor wanted nothing more than to spend the rest of his life getting to know this woman better and proving to her that love could be both tender and passionate.

Curling his body around hers, Seb considered all he had to lose if things did not turn around for him soon. He'd known the risks when he'd accepted the covert mission for the Texas Cattleman's Club that prevented him from providing the alibi that would clear his name. Still, the thought of forsaking his own heart for a higher principle couldn't keep a man warm in prison.

Seb tightened his grip around Susan and vowed somehow to find a way of protecting the club without sacrificing himself in the process.

Seven

Susan awoke to the aroma of coffee and frying bacon. True to his word, Seb had not only stayed for breakfast but even appeared to be in the process of fixing it himself. He must have gone to the grocery store while she was sleeping, because Susan hadn't had more than a half-gallon of milk and a loaf of moldy bread in her refrigerator. She was deeply touched by his thoughtfulness. Who would have guessed a millionaire could cook the way he did? Both in the kitchen and the bedroom...

Having enjoyed good sex only occasionally before, Susan reveled in the aftermath of truly great sex. It had truly been a mind-boggling experience. Last night the world had seemed to extend no farther than Susan's skin. No fireworks display could compare to the explosions that had rocked her so completely and sent her spinning dangerously out of control. The memory alone was enough to make her moan with renewed longing for Seb's loving touch. Though her mother assured her that it wasn't enough to base a marriage on, Susan was sure that such intense physical pleasure would help any relationship over the rough spots.

The indentation on the pillow next to her was a sweet reminder that she had not just awakened from a dream too good to be true. Drawing his pillow close to her, Susan breathed deeply of his masculine scent and wished there was some way of bottling the heady fragrance. Then she would have something around to remind her of Seb once she became a distant memory to him and he was back to his glamorous, jet-setting life. After his acquittal...

Or after spending years in prison for a crime she was certain he did not commit. A crime he might pay for as a direct result of her lack of skill in the courtroom.

Self-pity was instantly swallowed by a sense of panic. What if she was unable to prove him innocent of the charges? The last two juries she'd faced had decided against her client, and in this particular case, she had even less to go on than in either of those. Susan didn't think she could live with herself if she failed this man. She wasn't sure she could ever get out of bed again if Seb was to disappear from her life for any reason whatsoever.

She pulled the pillow over her face to stifle her feelings, lest they somehow find voice and alert Seb to her fears. The last thing he needed right now was to discover his attorney unraveling. That sort of thing didn't tend to inspire confidence in clients, and right now Susan knew it was important to be strong for him, as well as for her.

"What have I done?" she mumbled into the pillow, punching it once for good measure.

"Hungry, sleepyhead?" a deep sexy voice asked from the doorway.

Bare-chested, Seb took her breath away.

"Uh-huh," she affirmed, covering herself with a sheet as she sat up in bed. "And after I satisfy my hunger, do you think we could have some breakfast?"

"You're incorrigible," he replied with a lazy grin. "This certainly is a side of you I've never seen before, Counselor. Just as soon as you sample the veritable feast I've prepared for you in the kitchen, I'd sure like to see more of it."

Smiling coyly, Susan lowered her sheet with all the suspense of a practiced striptease artist.

"More of this?" she asked, feeling naughty and playful and completely unlike her normal modest—boring?—self. From where this wanton woman had sprung was a mystery, but judging by Seb's reaction, she would definitely have to bring her out more often.

"Well," he said, knitting his eyebrows and tapping his brow as if actually thinking it over, "seeing as you do have a microwave to heat my fine cuisine up later, I cast a vote for breakfast in bed."

With that, he took a flying leap onto the bed amid gales of feminine giggles. It had been so long since Susan had heard that unfettered sound from herself that she almost didn't recognize it. She was certain that no woman could feel self-conscious when her partner made sex so downright fun—and so very, very good. Between the laughter and her cries of passion, Susan was sure the neighbors were at a loss as to who had replaced the staid lawyer who used to live next door to them.

And just as soon as Susan figured it out herself, she'd be sure to let them know.

Even reheated in the microwave, breakfast was a delicious indulgence of the senses. In fact, Susan couldn't remember when food had tasted any better or, for that matter, when she had felt more ravenous about life itself. When she said as much to Seb, he grew suddenly earnest.

"What do you think about sampling my cooking every day?" he asked.

The thought of what he might actually be proposing made Susan's heart pound and her hands shake. Gulping air like a fish on the shore, she dismissed the possibility as ridiculous. Aside from the fact that he'd only known her a short while, she didn't see herself fitting in with the ultrawealthy crowd with whom he rubbed elbows on a regular basis. Not to mention that there were, at present, murder charges standing between Seb and his immediate future.

Reaching for the last piece of bacon, she strived to sound nonchalant over the thunderous beating of her heart. "What do you mean?"

"I want you to move in with me, Susan," he said, looking her right in the eye.

He reached across the table to take both her hands into his, and she felt the familiar zing of his touch settling into the most intimate zones of a body still humming with the aftereffects of their lovemaking.

"Are you serious?" Susan managed to ask without somehow choking on her food. Even in a state of shock, she was struck by the strength in the hands that caressed hers. And by their gentleness.

"I am," he assured her, pinning her with a gaze so intense and hot it sent her pulse fluttering out of control. The usual twinkle was gone from his eyes. Nothing about his manner indicated he was joking.

"Look," he went on, "as lovely as your place is, it seems a little...small for the two of us. I'm sure you could find a room or two at my house to designate as an office of sorts to contain all your paperwork, and I promise to feed you well. You did say that you like my cooking, didn't you? And Rosa is an even better cook than I am."

Susan's head swam. Having just recently gained her freedom, she wasn't sure she wanted to give it up just yet. Aside from the fact that they hadn't known each other very long, she had her professional reputation to consider. Not to mention her shell-shocked heart. Nor had she been raised to believe in simply shacking up with someone, rather than making the kind of lifetime commitment her parents had upheld every day for the past thirty-eight years. Of course, she hadn't been taught that divorce was acceptable, either. Or premarital sex, for that matter. And she could not bring herself to regret the intimacy they had shared even one little bit.

For lack of a better reason to refuse such a tempting offer, she blurted out, "What would people think?"

PLAY

7

Lucky

7 7 7

and you can get

FREE BOOKS AND
A FREE GIFT!

PLAY LUCKY 7 and get FREE Gifts!

7 Lucky

HOW TO PLAY:

1. With a coin, carefully scratch off the gold area at the right. Then check the claim chart to see what we have for you — **2 FREE BOOKS** and a **FREE GIFT** — **ALL YOURS FREE!**

2. Send back the card and you'll receive two brand-new Silhouette Desire® novels. These books have a cover price of $3.99 each in the U.S. and $4.50 each in Canada, but they are yours to keep absolutely free.

3. There's no catch. You're under no obligation to buy anything. We charge nothing — **ZERO** — for your first shipment. And you don't have to make any minimum number of purchases — not even one!

4. The fact is, thousands of readers enjoy receiving books by mail from the Silhouette Reader Service®. They enjoy the convenience of home delivery...they like getting the best new novels at discount prices, BEFORE they're available in stores...and they love their *Heart to Heart* subscriber newsletter featuring author news, horoscopes, recipes, book reviews and much more!

5. We hope that after receiving your free books you'll want to remain a subscriber. But the choice is yours — to continue or cancel, any time at all! So why not take us up on our invitation, with no risk of any kind. You'll be glad you did!

We can't tell you what it is...but we're sure you'll like it! A surprise **FREE GIFT** just for playing LUCKY 7!

Visit us online at
www.eHarlequin.com

NO COST! NO OBLIGATION TO BUY!

NO PURCHASE NECESSARY!

Scratch off the gold area with a coin. Then check below to see the gifts you get!

Lucky 7

YES! I have scratched off the gold area. Please send me the 2 Free books and gift for which I qualify. I understand I am under no obligation to purchase any books as explained on the back and on the opposite page.

326 SDL DNKR   225 SDL DNKL

FIRST NAME   LAST NAME

ADDRESS

APT.#   CITY

STATE/PROV.   ZIP/POSTAL CODE   (S-D-04/02)

7 7 7	Worth **2 FREE BOOKS** plus a **FREE GIFT!**
cherries	Worth **2 FREE BOOKS!**
clubs	Worth **1 FREE BOOK!**
bell	Try Again!

Offer limited to one per household and not valid to current Silhouette Desire® subscribers. All orders subject to approval.

DETACH AND MAIL CARD TODAY!

© 2001 HARLEQUIN ENTERPRISES LTD. ® and TM are trademarks owned by Harlequin Books S.A. used under license.

The Silhouette Reader Service® — Here's how it works:

Accepting your 2 free books and gift places you under no obligation to buy anything. You may keep the books and gift and return the shipping statement marked "cancel." If you do not cancel, about a month later we'll send you 6 additional books and bill you just $3.34 each in the U.S., or $3.74 each in Canada, plus 25¢ shipping & handling per book and applicable taxes if any.* That's the complete price and — compared to cover prices of $3.99 each in the U.S. and $4.50 each in Canada — it's quite a bargain! You may cancel at any time, but if you choose to continue, every month we'll send you 6 more books, which you may either purchase at the discount price or return to us and cancel your subscription.

*Terms and prices subject to change without notice. Sales tax applicable in N.Y. Canadian residents will be charged applicable provincial taxes and GST.

If offer card is missing write to: Silhouette Reader Service, 3010 Walden Ave., P.O. Box 1867, Buffalo NY 14240-1867

BUSINESS REPLY MAIL
FIRST-CLASS MAIL   PERMIT NO. 717-003   BUFFALO, NY

POSTAGE WILL BE PAID BY ADDRESSEE

SILHOUETTE READER SERVICE
3010 WALDEN AVE
PO BOX 1867
BUFFALO NY 14240-9952

NO POSTAGE
NECESSARY
IF MAILED
IN THE
UNITED STATES

"Who cares?" Seb rejoined with the kind of candor and indifference to the opinion of the masses that had made him such a phenomenal success in business. "I want to know what *you* think, Susan."

Looking into the face of the man who made her feel more desirable and cherished than anyone ever had before, Susan felt hope well up inside her. She felt like a songbird watching the door of its cage being unlocked and opened wide. Released from the bars that kept it earthbound, it did not hesitate to break into a joyous tune. And if, like poor Icarus in the Greek myth, the bird were to singe its wings by flying too close to the sun and ultimately be hurled onto the stones, there was an irrefutable splendor in its attempt to soar to heaven.

"I think you're crazy," Susan told him truthfully.

"I am," Sebastian assured her, caressing her hands tenderly and drawing them to a cheek rough with the stubble that had grown there overnight. "Crazy about you."

His words were balm for a wounded spirit still leery of becoming romantically involved again. Experience had taught Susan caution. She had been thoroughly taken in by the charming facade that Joe had presented to her and to the world while he was wooing her. It was not until after she was wearing his ring that she discovered the cruel, controlling nature behind that smiling mask. Torn between fear of making yet another disastrous mistake and the desire to give love a second chance, she hoped to have a safety net securely in place before she took another leap of faith—as if there was such a thing as safety nets when it came to matters of the heart.

"I suppose such an arrangement would make working together a whole lot easier," she conceded. "You're not exactly the easiest person to get hold of, and rather than trying to hunt you down a dozen times a day, this way I'd be sure to see you at least in the mornings and evenings. I assume that I would have faster access to any information I'd need if we were staying together."

The smile that spread across Seb's face was broad and genuine. It encompassed a world of possibilities. Susan's implication that this arrangement would be temporary, based on the need to work on his case, did not dampen his obvious delight at her tentative concurrence.

"Of course, I want to keep my apartment," she added, not about to give up her safe haven in case things didn't work out.

"Whatever you think, Counselor," Sebastian agreed, kissing her senseless.

The sense of urgency he displayed in committing her to the move gave Susan the distinct impression that he was worried she might change her mind if he gave her another second to think about it.

"Let me help you get started packing," he said, grabbing a phone and putting things in motion before she had a chance to protest.

There was an unnerving sense of déjà vu about the process of moving into Seb's home. As much as Susan would like to repress the memory altogether, his take-charge manner reminded her of the way Joe had hustled her into marriage. There was solace in the fact that if things turned sour in her relationship with

Sebastian, no messy divorce would complicate her leaving whenever she wanted.

Why that thought made her feel sad rather than reassured was a mystery to her.

Moving in with a millionaire had certain advantages, in any event. Having sacrificed most of her material possessions in her divorce as a means of appeasing Joe and being rid of him as quickly as possible, Susan didn't have a whole lot left to her name. A moving company Seb hired before he took off for work loaded up her meager belongings in no time at all. By afternoon she was moved lock, stock and barrel into Seb's veritable mansion. It wasn't until she was standing at the doorway all alone that Susan realized the full import of what she had done.

She felt rather like Cinderella returning after the ball, minus the fancy party dress. Having taken the day off to accommodate this oh-so-impetuous decision, she was wearing clothing appropriate for moving day. Dressed in a pair of faded jeans and a dusty white cotton shirt, she wondered if she should knock on the door of her new residence or simply barge right in. Would she be mistaken as a salesperson and shooed away before she had a chance to explain herself? For that matter, would she ever feel at ease in a house with more rooms than her entire apartment complex?

She was on the verge of bolting when an older Spanish woman opened the door. Her dark hair was sprinkled with gray, and her dark eyes smiled a welcome that instantly made Susan feel less out of place.

"You must be Susan," the woman said, looking her over from top to toe in one sweeping glance that missed nothing. "Come in, come in. I've been expecting you."

Silently Susan thanked Seb for his thoughtfulness in alerting the staff of her arrival. No matter that she undoubtedly looked far plainer and more unsophisticated than his usual lady friends—she felt almost at ease. What could have been a terribly awkward moment took on the feel of a homecoming.

"You must be exhausted," the woman continued, gesturing for Susan to follow. Once inside, she stuck out her hand and introduced herself. "I'm Rosa."

Susan liked Rosa immediately. Her callused hands reminded Susan of her mother, as did the strong grasp that belied her slight stature. Her English was excellent.

"Seb speaks fondly of you," Susan said, recalling his fear of displeasing this woman by leaving too much of a mess behind when he'd barbecued the other evening. This brief personal introduction made her understand why.

"He is like a son to me," Rosa replied simply.

Though her words didn't sound like a warning, Susan suspected this demure, grandmotherly housekeeper would be capable of the ferocity of a tiger when its cub was threatened.

"You're the lawyer who is going to clear my Sebbie's name, is that not right?" Rosa asked, peering at the new houseguest suspiciously.

Susan smiled, wondering how Seb would react if she was to use the same fond childhood endearment. She knew she didn't look much like a lawyer at the moment and hoped Rosa didn't think she was merely some gold digger out to cut herself a fat deal at the expense of her client.

"I'm certainly going to do my best to get that result," she replied. "If you don't mind designating a room for me to use as my office while I'm here, I'd like to get started setting things up right away."

The quizzical look on Rosa's face gave the impression that she thought poor Seb must have picked her up at a blue light litigation special. Susan hastened to explain.

"Don't worry. I won't be underfoot much at all, and I'll do my best to stay out of your way. I have a regular office downtown. It's just that I plan on bringing a lot of work home with me, and I don't want to be running back and forth any more than I have to."

Rosa looked pleased.

"You strike me as a sensible girl," she said. "Not like those society bimbos who want to be waited on hand and foot and spoon-fed their caviar. I expect you'll do well enough by Sebbie."

Susan assumed the housekeeper was referring to her legal services, but she wasn't completely sure. Nonetheless, she was warmed by the compliment. Rosa continued in her matter-of-fact manner, "Dinner will be ready at seven. Seb should be home before then, unless he's told you anything different."

Glad that she had no information to upset the woman's plans, Susan shook her head.

"Then why don't you go on upstairs and pick out as many of the extra rooms as you want and make yourself comfortable? If you need anything, just let me know."

Susan started for the stairs, but was stopped before she had taken three full steps.

"You do believe that he's innocent, don't you?" Rosa asked point-blank.

Susan didn't hesitate to respond just as earnestly as Rosa had inquired. "I wouldn't be representing him if I didn't believe that. However, proving it to people who don't know him like we do may be harder than either you or I would like to believe."

Blessing herself with the sign of the cross, the older woman called on a higher power to support the cause of the unfairly accused. "I have faith in God," she said, gesturing upward. "And in you."

Susan took comfort in Rosa's words. She desperately hoped she could live up to this woman's expectations. With renewed determination, she vowed to go through the case yet again to see if there was any detail she had possibly overlooked that might shed some light on the real murderer. Before she left, however, Rosa asked her a final question that left Susan pondering the housekeeper's motives.

"Say, how do you feel about children?"

Eight

Susan had never been more deliriously happy in her life.

Or more terrified.

Her nights and evenings were spent in the company of a man who made her laugh one minute and cry out in ecstasy the next. Sebastian Wescott was the wildest, most wonderful roller-coaster ride she had ever had the privilege to take. It was all she could do to hang on. He was teaching her things in bed that would make her mother blush, all the while making her feel like the most desirable and passionate woman on the face of the earth. That his tenderness extended beyond the boundaries of his bedroom meant more to her than she could put into words. Every day he made a point of making her feel special and listening to her as if whatever she had to say was important and fascinating. He had also taken to sending her flowers every day and tucking love notes in her briefcase.

Susan was thankful that Seb wasn't pushing for any commitment beyond their living together. This arrangement gave her the perfect opportunity to discern any sign of the kind of Jekyll-and-Hyde personality that Joe had kept so well hidden until after they were married. Susan was relieved to discover that for all his intensity on the job, Seb was easygoing and relaxed during his off-hours. He claimed that he had learned early on to distinguish between home and work out of fear of becoming just like the father he despised.

Susan was having a more difficult time separating her personal and professional life. Though her nights were spent in rapture, her days were occupied with legal briefs, stacks of growing paperwork and the grinding process of subpoenaing anyone and everyone who just might be able to shed light on a way to clear Seb's name if the grand jury actually handed down an indictment. It was a time-consuming and arduous process that so far had turned up little in the way of hard evidence. For her time, she had accomplished little more than compiling a list of witnesses a mile long who were just itching to vouch for Seb's character as a boss, a philanthropist and a hero dating clear back to his stint in the military. Unfortunately such testimony held little weight in light of the evidence piling up against him.

Susan had yet to pin down his alibi for the night of the murder. Seb's earlier evasiveness had turned into outright refusal to shed any light on his where-

abouts on the evening in question. She supposed she
should be glad that he refused to simply invent an
alibi. But Susan couldn't convince Seb how critical
this information would be in procuring his freedom.
It was worrisome, to say the least.

Susan was relieved to discover that Dorian's as-
sessment of his half brother's standing among the
ranks of his employees was 180 degrees off. The fact
that disgruntled employees were few and far between
was a tribute to Seb's management style, but it didn't
help a bit in uncovering a motive for setting the boss
up in such an insidious manner. So far every single
lead she had turned up ultimately had dead-ended,
leaving Susan more frustrated with each passing day.

The closer she got to Seb personally, the more
intensely she redoubled her efforts to prove him innocent. The crux of the prosecution's case was a
damaging e-mail supposedly sent by Seb himself in
which he appeared so incensed by the discovery that
Eric had been misappropriating company funds that
he actually threatened to kill him. Seb had dryly
pointed out that it was not a particularly bright move
for the CEO of a major international corporation to
put such a thing in writing, but the police were not
smiling. To make matters worse, Robert Cole, the
private detective that Sebastian himself had hired to
find the murderer, was the one who had uncovered
evidence in Seb's own office tying him to the missing money.

Granted, the evidence was circumstantial, but it
was damaging nonetheless. Other men had been convicted on far less. Susan knew that unless she came
up with something fast, they were headed for trial

armed with little more than pluck and an endless supply of character witnesses. When Seb offered his extended legal services from the staff he kept on retainer, Susan gladly accepted his help. As much as she would have liked the honor of being his sole legal representative, there was too much at stake to let silly pride get in the way of good sense. Seb looked relieved when she put up no fight. Buried in paperwork back at the office, Ann heartily agreed.

"Now that the word's out that you're representing Sebastian Wescott, we have more clients lined up than you could shake a fat stick at," her assistant reported gleefully over the phone.

"I'm afraid you'll have to put them all on hold until this mess is behind us," Susan told her with a sigh.

"They'll be back."

Ann sounded certain about that, but Susan wasn't so sure.

"Not if we don't win."

The implications of that statement hung in the air like the very telephone line that transmitted it. When Ann spoke again, it was in a more solemn and personal tone.

"Listen, right now our mutual financial future doesn't worry me half as much as your emotional state. Why don't you just drop the pretense and answer me—how *are* you?"

"Wonderful," Susan admitted with a girlish tone that she knew was a tip-off to the early stages of lovesickness. "And terrible," she added half a moment later, putting voice to her wild fluctuations between bliss and panic. "I've finally found the man of my dreams, and I'm afraid there isn't anything I can do to keep him from being convicted and thrown in prison for a crime I know he didn't do.''

Ann's assurances that love would find a way and that things would surely work out in the end weren't all that comforting. They were the same kind of platitudes that Rosa was fond of mouthing. At least Seb's loyal housekeeper backed hers up with a barrage of prayers.

In the short time she had been living at the mansion, Susan had come to respect Rosa and enjoy her company. Aside from making the best fajitas in the entire state of Texas, the older woman was a wealth of information. Outspoken and opinionated, she seemed impressed when Susan insisted on helping her prepare dinner whenever she could spare the time. Just as Seb had suspected, she approved of Susan's blue-collar roots and lack of pretense.

"For a lawyer, you're pretty handy in the kitchen," she remarked. "And," she added, grabbing the cutting board, "you're certainly a much nicer houseguest than that phony-baloney Dorian."

The way Rosa spat out the man's name made Susan wonder what he could possibly have done to have gotten so firmly entrenched on Rosa's bad side. She soon heard more on the subject as the housekeeper chopped up onions and Dorian's moral fiber with equal relish. Apparently when Dorian had first arrived in town, Seb had taken him into his own home until he could find something suitable in town. According to Rosa, the man outstayed his welcome the very first week and stayed on way past any respectable amount of time to get his feet under him.

Susan didn't dare ask what the religiously devout older woman thought of her living arrangement with Seb. Although Rosa never made mention of it, Susan suspected her beliefs were quite similar to those her own parents held so dear. All those Sundays they'd dragged their boisterous brood to church hadn't been just because they liked getting all dressed up once a week.

Susan kept on peeling the potatoes without adding much other than her presence to the conversation.

"Thought I should wait on him hand and foot, that one did," Rosa continued her tirade against Seb's half brother. "Acted like he was entitled to everything Sebastian has worked his whole life to build up and overcome just because his daddy planted seeds in every field he passed. You look close and you'll see jealousy in Dorian's eyes that no amount of charity is going to wipe away. Mark my words, he fancies himself the lord of the manor. I told Sebastian that it wasn't his responsibility to pay for his father's mistakes, but that boy doesn't listen any better now than when he was twelve. He's headstrong, all right, but you won't find a man with a truer heart anywhere. He'll make some woman a fine husband some day."

Ignoring the sidelong glance Rosa shot her way, Susan pretended to focus all her attention on the growing mound of potato peelings. The dear woman was as subtle as an elephant doing the cakewalk. Still, Susan couldn't help but love her in spite of her meddling nature. Though Susan herself had quickly become disenchanted with Dorian, she couldn't imagine what he had done to make someone as kind-hearted as Rosa so thoroughly dislike him.

''Just as soon as this case is put to bed and Seb's cleared of all charges, I expect the two of you will start making plans. I do hope they include having children.''

The potato peeler clattered into the sink. Red-faced, Susan mumbled something about not being able to stand the heat as she hastened to get the heck out of the kitchen.

The Wescott estate was awash in the colors of spring. Susan found the humble crab-apple trees the most striking as she took a walk with the intention of clearing her head. They reminded her of prim old ladies, who, though plain and proper most of the year, donned bonnets of shocking purple, hoping to outdo one another at Eastertime. All too soon a big wind was bound to strip them of their glory, but for an instant the splendor of youth was upon them.

Walking hand in hand with Seb through the well-tended grounds, Susan felt a serenity that was rare in her hectic lifestyle. The weather was becoming warm enough that most days a sweater could be substituted for a heavier jacket. It hadn't taken Susan long to discover that getting used to this way of life was a whole lot easier than she thought. Six days out of seven Rosa prepared delicious, wholesome meals, and Seb took particular delight in barbecuing on her day off. Though Susan protested that she was gaining weight, the truth was, she had never looked better in her life.

She found herself looking forward to sharing the

day's events with Seb every evening when he returned home from work. Daily walks and creative excursions provided time to unwind. Susan had not known it possible to feel so comfortable and fulfilled in a relationship. Had it not been for the ghastly accusation hanging over them like a gathering storm, life would have been nothing short of perfect.

Susan hesitated to bring up anything that would ruin their idyllic outing, but there was little point in postponing the inevitable. Earlier in the day she had spoken to a friend at the county attorney's office, who told her that while not airtight, the case they were building against Susan's client was sound enough to warrant taking it to the grand jury. If Seb didn't stop sidestepping her inquiries about the night in question, Susan held out little hope that she could keep him from an indictment. For all the boldness he displayed regarding his faith in her abilities, she hoped this news would shake him from his sense of blithe optimism.

She pulled Seb off the path and over to a picturesque bench. "We need to talk," she told him as he took a seat beside her. "Look, I know you're under the belief that you can't be indicted on circumstantial evidence alone and that because you're innocent, justice will automatically prevail. I hate to be the one to tell you this, but that isn't always the case. To be blunt, things are looking pretty bleak as far as your case is concerned. Aside from that questionable e-mail sent under your name, the recent discovery of money being funneled into a private account in your name is more than enough to warrant an indictment."

Seb refused to believe it. "Why can't anyone see I'm being framed? Don't you think the fact that my own investigator turned up that juicy little bit of information makes it suspect?"

"It doesn't matter what I think," she insisted, doing her best to drive her point home. "As far as I can tell right now, the only thing that will appease the grand jury is a verifiable alibi for you on the night of the murder. I need your help on this. All you've told me is that you were out of town. You have to tell me where you were and what you were doing."

Just as Susan expected, Seb balked at the request. His eyes grew sad and his muscles taut as he responded in the same evasive way he did every time she put the question to him. "I've already told you that I'm not at liberty to talk about that night."

"Why not?" Susan snapped. If she was weary of his sidestepping, she could only imagine what a jury would make of it. "I can't think of anything so terrible that would be worth your freedom. As your lawyer, I'm bound by law to keep what you tell me confidential, and you have to know I would do absolutely nothing to jeopardize your case. As your lover, I have to tell you I don't like having secrets between us."

"I don't, either," Seb retorted angrily. "The only thing I like less is feeling I don't have your trust."

"That's not fair," Susan countered, her own frustration apparent in the way her eyes darkened at the accusation. "Obviously it's you who doesn't trust me."

Tension crackled between them. The issue could no longer be avoided, and neither one wanted to walk away from their first fight without making their individual positions crystal clear. Sunset faded. The sky darkened as twilight settled in around them.

"If I didn't trust you, would I have made you my lead attorney when I could have hired any criminal lawyer in Texas?"

The point softened Susan. She was truly grateful for the opportunity to represent him, but not so much that she was willing to let him go on disregarding her need for full disclosure. His testimony was crucial; to a jury, it would seem tantamount to a guilty plea to plead the Fifth in a murder case.

"Whatever happened that night, I'd like to think we can work it out together. All I'm asking is for you to put your faith in us—in me." The intensity of her emotions could not be ignored. She might as well have handed him her heart on a platter.

Sebastian splayed his fingers through his hair, sparking glints of red in the thatch of chestnut brown. "How about you having some faith in me?" His voice sounded equally troubled. "Can't you believe there are some things worth the sacrifice of one's personal freedom, or are you actually starting to question my innocence, too, Counselor?"

Susan didn't answer him right away. She didn't believe the man with whom she was falling hopelessly in love was capable of cold-blooded murder. Still, she could not understand why he so adamantly refused to provide an alibi for himself. Her mind ran rampant with possibilities. None of them advanced his case—or the possibility of a lasting relationship between the two of them.

She was just about to tell him as much when her worst fears were realized.

A police car pulled into the driveway.

A moment later an officer approached the two of them. "I'm sorry to interrupt your evening, Mr. Wescott but we need you to come down to the station to answer a few more questions."

"Why?" Susan was quick to ask. "As his lawyer I'd like to know what's so important that it couldn't wait until morning."

The officer shook his head. "I can't say, other than that new evidence has come to light."

Taking Seb's hand into her own, Susan squeezed hard. Whatever her personal doubts might be, it was crucial they present a united front to the law.

"Don't worry," she said with a brave, albeit wobbly, smile. "You don't have to face this alone."

Nine

Why Susan would be having such an erotic dream on the heels of such a fitful night's sleep was beyond all understanding, but she wasn't about to question a good thing, whether in a conscious or unconscious state. It would have been too easy to blame her sensations on the navy satin sheets and chenille bedding that so typified her absent lover: totally masculine in its luxurious indulgence. It was not the bedding, however, that had kept her awake half the night. Funny how in such a short time she had grown so used to sleeping with Seb that falling asleep without him had become nigh onto impossible. A satin pillow made a poor substitute for a warm and willing body.

After accompanying Sebastian downtown to the police station last night, she had remained in his presence throughout the questioning process. She was glad to have been there. Outraged at being hauled into jail for more questioning like some common criminal, he was in no mood to frame his answers in tactful, legally appropriate jargon. More than once, his temper flared.

It was all Susan could do to keep him under control. The timing and antagonistic method that the investigating officer employed was clearly a deliberate tactic intended first to catch her client off guard and then bait him. She cringed when Sebastian flippantly told the man that where he was the night of the murder was none of his damned business. Had she not been there to intervene, Susan suspected Sebastian would be up on charges of assaulting an officer to boot.

His aggressive posturing had done little but reinforce the assertion that he was a dangerous character. In fact, he was so angry by the time the police finished questioning him that Seb had refused to accompany Susan home, saying only that he needed some time alone to think. He'd also refused her offer of help when he told her he was going back to the office to search through his records once more to see if he could figure out how account records for an account he had never set up had been saved in his personal computer files.

Knowing better than to argue with Seb when he was in such a determined mood, Susan had gone back to the house, crawled into a lonesome bed and cried herself to sleep.

None of that mattered at the moment. Not when her dream man was feathering kisses along the nape of her neck. Goose bumps marked his path. Susan was tempted to roll over onto her back and see where that led him, but she didn't want to risk rousing herself from such a delightful phantasm. The daring fellow stopped only long enough to divest her of her covers before proceeding to trail more kisses down her bare back. Since moving in with Seb, Susan had taken to sleeping in the nude, a fact her fantasy lover seemed to appreciate just as much as his flesh-and-blood counterpart. So vivid was this dream that she thought she even sensed Seb's distinctive scent in the air. Like him, it was thoroughly masculine and as stimulating as pure musk.

Susan breathed him deeply into her lungs.

A gentle nudge parted her legs. Magic hands rubbed her buttocks with a languid, practiced touch. Lost in hedonistic pleasure, Susan moaned aloud, then gasped as strong fingers slipped inside and turned her to liquid fire. The world began and ended in the secret core of her being.

Throbbing, she dared not pull away from such an exquisite indulgence of her senses. Dream or not, she was slick and ready with wanting and on the verge of achieving a very real climax. A whisper in her ear encouraged her to let go and simply enjoy his gift to her. Burrowing deeper into her pillow, she called out Seb's name as if hoping to somehow conjure him up from the world of the ethereal to the material.

"I'm right here."

That voice did not sound at all disembodied and so startled her that Susan felt compelled to lift her head from her pillow. There was no denying that she had been working way too hard lately, but she certainly hadn't expected her body to respond to the demands she put on it by plunging her so completely into an imaginary world. Not that her hallucinations didn't beat reality all to pieces.

Susan blinked hard as she propped herself up on her elbows. She wanted with all her might to believe her eyes. Seb was here. Actually and physically present. Stripped down to his bare skin, he was clearly as aroused as she was.

"It's a good thing you didn't call out some other man's name," he said.

His silver eyes glistened wickedly.

Susan had a million questions she wanted to ask him, but right now she couldn't think of a single one. Not when her body was begging for release. Seb seemed in no hurry to provide any explanation for his presence, either. He was too intent on the naked woman squirming beneath him.

Grabbing for the bars of the brass headboard, Susan implored him to share her bliss. He needed little coaxing. She whimpered as he lowered his weight on her and the two became one.

That body and soul could meld in such a seamless expression of passion was a source of never-ending wonder to Susan. That the summit was in plain sight made the view nonetheless breathtaking. Tightening her grip on the headboard, Susan let go of all her inhibitions. She had no control over the animallike noises she was making. They sounded foreign and faraway as the passion steadily building in intensity created a roaring in her head that drowned out everything else. Her cries resonated throughout the room as they reached the top together in an explosion that left her trembling.

Carefully removing his weight from her, Sebastian rolled her over and proceeded to kiss her with such tenderness it made tears rise to her eyes.

"I love you," he said simply.

Teardrops perfect as diamonds rolled down Susan's face. Wrapping her arms around Seb's broad shoulders, she held her heart against his so that it seemed they beat as one. Spoken aloud, those words had the capacity to dislodge all of her lingering fears about their relationship being based on sex alone. Those sweet words acted as a magic wand to remove all the obstacles Susan had ever imagined keeping them apart.

"I love you, too," she whispered fiercely.

Coming from her lips, Susan hoped those same words had the power to dissolve any secrets between them. She could not believe that God would be so cruel as to take this man from her now that she was committed to him both body and soul. Surely love alone could conquer whatever lay ahead of them. Overcome with a feeling of euphoria, she snuggled against Seb's warm body, drifting back to sleep safe in the circle of his loving arms.

Having been interrupted once before due to bad timing, Susan waited until well after brunch before again broaching the subject of Seb's failure to provide an alibi. Stepping into his den, she took the phone off the hook and handed him an important-looking document.

"What's this?" he asked.

Words felt like rocks in her mouth.

"Official notification of your preliminary hearing."

Seb swore softly. "So it's actually come to this, has it?" he muttered.

"I'm afraid so."

As much as she hated breaking such bad news to him, Susan hoped it would at last make him understand the seriousness of his situation. Surely now he would feel compelled to provide her with an alibi for the night of the murder. Whoever or whatever he was protecting was hardly worth the loss of his independence and personal integrity. Committed as they were to each other, Susan expected him to put their relationship before all others. Once this matter was resolved, she assumed that marriage was the next logical step.

Unfortunately Sebastian didn't see things that way at all.

"I've told you over and over again that I can't tell you about what happened that night, Susan."

His tone held a note of frustration, and his face took on a stubborn look Susan had come to know only too well. She didn't bother arguing the merits of her request on the basis of the law. Instead, she addressed him on a far more personal level, not bothering to hide her distress.

"What could possibly be more important than our relationship?" she wanted to know. "Or do you actually expect me to wait for an explanation until you're released from prison? Do you really think we can pick up our lives twenty some years from now and go on as if nothing ever happened?"

Sorrow settled about Sebastian like a shroud. "No,

sweetheart, I most certainly don't expect anyone as young and beautiful and vibrant as you to waste your life waiting on me. A woman like you deserves to have a normal life and a house full of rowdy kids who absolutely adore their mother and respect their father. If the worst happens and I end up doing time, I want you to pretend you never met me. Though for me, forgetting you would be like forgetting how to breathe—you're that much a part of who I am.''

Susan wanted to hit him. The man refused to fight fair. Setting aside the tender feelings his words evoked in her, she wound up and gave him her best shot.

''This whole issue is about trust. Lack of trust was what killed my marriage. Joe didn't trust me to choose my own friends, run my own business or know my own mind. He had no faith in me. He demanded that I check in with him before I went anywhere and report back on any interactions I had outside of his presence. His idea of protecting me was to keep me in the dark about everything from his business transactions to the amount of money available in our checking account to whom he was keeping company with. I get the feeling that your reticence with me is more about your lack of confidence in my skills as an attorney than it is about upholding some secret, sacred honor.''

''You couldn't be more wrong,'' he told her, wishing there was some way to make her believe him.

''Be honest, Seb, isn't that why you put your entire legal team at my disposal?''

''No, it isn't. I simply thought you could use the

help. Face it, even Superwoman couldn't be expected to handle a case of this magnitude all by herself.''

Susan was in no mood to listen to logic. Her heart was telling her that something was mightily wrong, and she intended to get to the bottom of it without further ado. She put her hands on her hips as he continued speaking.

''All I can tell you is that a man is only as good as his word. If I were to violate the principles I solemnly swore to uphold, I wouldn't be fit for you to live with—or to live with myself, for that matter.''

Susan was clearly nettled. ''Whatever you're talking about sounds an awful lot like the kind of top-secret club my brothers formed in our backyard when they were twelve. I ripped up that Boys Only sign they posted on my playhouse way back then, and I'll have you know I won't stand for it now.''

Angry at being pushed into a corner, Seb went on the offensive. Again Susan was reminded of the caged panther he had resembled, pacing back and forth in front of her office desk, the very first time they met.

''You're right about one thing and one thing only,'' he told her, his voice deepening to a growl. ''This is about trust. If I say I'm innocent, that should be good enough for someone who claims to love me. As far as I'm concerned, true love shouldn't have to be substantiated by legal briefs, depositions or written explanations in triplicate. My word should damn well be enough, Susan.''

''If you truly love me, you could tell me where you were and what you were doing that night. Period.''

Not one to ever issue rash ultimatums, Susan trembled at the magnitude of that statement. She was as keenly aware that this was a turning point in their relationship as she was of the sudden drop in temperature. Outside the big picture window where Sebastian stood with arms crossed over his chest, clouds shaped like rain buckets blew in, and a gust of wind scattered a profusion of apple blossoms across the sky. The sight brought to mind flower girls dropping pink petals along the aisle of the wedding Susan had secretly hoped for but now realized was never meant to be.

"Obviously we've reached a stalemate," Seb said.

As much as Susan admired him for refusing to back down under pressure, she could not forgive him for letting them both down because of a fool's code of honor. Was there no way to make him see the cost of such stubborn male pride?

"You can call it checkmate if you want and declare yourself the winner, for all I care."

Susan's voice cracked right down the middle—like her heart. Imagining its blood-red fragments fluttering among the pale petals surrealistically suspended in the space that was to separate them forever, she was determined to have the last word.

"If you're going to take that attitude, you'll have to find yourself another lawyer. I quit."

Ten

It was raining when Susan moved out of the Wescott mansion. The pattering of drops on the roof echoed the beat of her aching heart and mirrored the tears she saw welling up in Rosa's kind brown eyes. Saying goodbye to that gentle woman was harder than she could have imagined. In the short time Susan had lived there, they had become close.

"I'm going to miss your mothering," she said, giving the Spanish woman a big hug.

Rosa smelled of pungent spices and talcum powder. Strong, plump arms encircled Susan and held her tight. It was with regret that Rosa finally released her. She had made no secret of hoping to hold one of Susan and Sebastian's babies in her arms before the year was out. She had often pointed out that the children of such a union would surely be good-looking and smart.

"Pride makes a lonely bedfellow," Rosa admonished, lifting a tissue to her watery eyes.

"Try telling that to Seb," Susan told her.

She felt instantly repentant for the tone if not the intent of her words. This woman had been nothing but kind to her, and Susan had not meant to bark at her. She did not want to sever their friendship just because Sebastian Wescott was too big a fool to see what his obstinacy was costing him. Taking Rosa's work-roughened hands into her own, Susan squeezed them warmly. If Seb had but one-tenth of the confidence that his housekeeper put in her ability to represent him, Susan would have gladly worked her fingers to the bone in his defense.

"Take good care of him," she said, trying hard to force the words through the tightening of her throat.

Susan left as she had come, with little more than a suitcase and several boxes of papers associated with the case. She left behind only her heart and a note indicating that she would be more than happy to turn over all she had to the attorney of his choice. Despite the bitterness between them, she was far more concerned about Sebastian's welfare than the fact that she was facing financial ruin. Businesses could be rebuilt, after all, especially if one was willing to relocate and start all over again.

But bankrupt hearts were another matter altogether.

The windshield wiper on the driver's side of her car wasn't working correctly. Susan was nonetheless grateful for the steady drizzle that continued throughout the night. It provided good cover for the tears that fell so freely down her face as her old blue Taurus found its way back home—that empty place where she had once taken respite from a world too restrictive. Opening the door to her apartment, Susan was struck by how barren and stark her living quarters were. And by how perfectly they reflected her life.

Leaving Joe had been far easier than leaving Seb. The former move had evoked a sense of freedom that had made Susan feel light and buoyant for months afterward. Today's departure had the exact opposite effect. Her bones felt encased in granite, and her aching heart seemed to have quadrupled in size.

Though it was long after midnight when she finally crawled into bed, it was hours before sleep claimed her. Even then, Sebastian haunted her dreams. Three times she awoke from a fitful vision, clutching a tear-soaked pillow, her sheets twisted tightly around her. She did not know whether waking up with his name on her lips was the result of a prayer or a curse.

Sunlight leaking through a far-off gap in the horizon was reason enough for Susan to forgo her lonely bed in the early hours of the morning. Tossing aside the covers, she turned off an alarm that had yet to ring and faced the day with grim resolve. Having fired herself from the only case that could possibly have salvaged her business—not to mention her faith in herself—Susan knew the only honorable thing to do was write her good friend and secretary, Ann, a glowing letter of recommendation and let her go.

Letting go was becoming Susan's specialty.

Rosa's words proved just as prophetic for Sebastian as they had for Susan. Unable to bear watching the woman he loved walk out of his life, Sebastian left home intending to spend the night in the private suite behind his office. His bed felt as big as all of Texas without Susan in it. All night long he rolled from one side to the other searching for an elusively restful position. It hadn't taken him long at all to grow accustomed to the warmth and comfort of Susan's body curled against him each and every night. A kitten couldn't cuddle more adorably than she did. Or purr any more contentedly when she was pleased.

He suspected it would take far longer to acclimate himself to an empty bed. In frustration, he turned on the big-screen television set in his suite, hoping to find anything that might induce sleep. Golf was usually a sure cure for insomnia. Not tonight. By the sixteenth hole, he pulled himself out of bed and headed for the fridge.

He immediately discovered how different food tasted in Susan's absence. With her, life was a banquet of strawberries dipped in warm, melted chocolate. Of fresh Alaskan king crab dripping with butter. Brownies marbled with rich cream cheese served hot from the oven. Sharp cheddar. The aroma of homemade bread baked to golden-brown perfection. Triple-deckered ice-cream cones melting on one's tongue. Exotic candies packaged in gold foil, each a surprise to be unwrapped and savored at length. With Susan every bite of life was delicious.

Without her everything tasted like plain soda crackers. Dry and flavorless. With nothing to wash them down.

Sebastian abandoned the imported caviar and champagne from his stock for a can of plain old domestic beer. The brand didn't matter. He only hoped the alcohol would dull the pain pulsing in his every cell.

The beer he downed while waiting for the sun to rise failed to do the trick, leaving him, instead, with a bear of a headache that no amount of aspirin could cure for what seemed like days on end. Slight noises drove him to distraction. The music of Susan's laughter was replaced by the incessant barking of dogs. The sound of Rosa's sorrowful "tsk, tsk, tsking" drove Sebastian away from home, as did the ghosts of happier times haunting his vast estate. Indeed, the sound of anyone's voice but Susan's so clearly irritated him that valued employees quickly learned it was far better to correspond with their boss via e-mail rather than face-to-face.

The note Susan had left providing instructions for a new lawyer to contact her office for the files on his case lay wadded in the garbage. Sebastian had no desire to replace her either in the bedroom or the courtroom. He might have initially hired Susan to represent him out of a peculiar mixture of sympathy and desire, but he had come to genuinely respect her abilities. If she couldn't find a way to get him off, he was convinced nobody could. He decided to put his faith in a justice system designed to protect the innocent, something to which he, too, had pledged his life.

If only there was some way of explaining to Susan that he could not disclose where he was on the night of Eric's murder without compromising the lives of two defenseless people—one a mere child. If protecting them, as well as upholding the honor of the

Texas Cattleman's Club itself, meant having to serve time in prison for a crime he did not commit, then so be it. Sebastian understood the magnitude of the oath he had sworn as a member of the club and would accept the consequences as a man of principle. What bothered Sebastian more than anything, even the thought of doing time, was that Susan was unable to accept him at his word. The thought that she might actually think him capable of cold-blooded murder left him completely bereft and indifferent to the possible incarceration that awaited him.

Susan stared at the files littering her office floor and bit her lip in consternation. She could not bring herself to believe the rumor that Sebastian Wescott actually intended to represent himself in court. Without someone to intervene on his behalf, she knew the prosecution would jab mercilessly at him once they had him on the stand until he eventually lost patience and gave the jury a display of his intimidating temper.

The thought made her physically ill. It only added to the speculation among some people around town that her sudden weight loss was due to diet pills. Others, noting the dark circles under her eyes, worried that she had contracted something fatal. Joe went so far as to send her a tongue-in-cheek get-well card, casually mentioning that the loss of her celebrated client was general knowledge all over town.

Susan simply couldn't let Sebastian represent himself. It was suicidal. Neither could she represent him under the conditions he set forth—adamantly refusing to provide her with his alibi for the night of the murder.

Either he trusted her or he didn't.

Either she loved him or she didn't.

Torn between heart and conscience, she decided to contact Dorian and see if he could make his stubborn half brother listen to reason. When she called to set up an appointment, Dorian apologized for being so busy but said he could squeeze in a few minutes for her at his workplace. As much as Susan hated the thought of running into Sebastian at the Wescott office building, she swallowed her pride and gratefully accepted Dorian's terms for their meeting.

Susan needn't have worried about any chance encounters with Sebastian. When she arrived, Marilyn Bachman, the secretary whose precocious little girl had taken off from school to spend the day with her earlier in the month, explained that Sebastian had taken a leave of absence. The thought of Sebastian's mammoth company running without him at the helm left her feeling as hopelessly adrift as his employees, who were doing their best to pretend that nothing was amiss.

As Susan expected, Dorian was completely sympathetic to her cause. He was looking exceptionally well. A single flake of dandruff stuck to the shoulder of his black turtleneck was the only thing amiss in his appearance. A matching pair of dark slacks and sunglasses gave him an upscale casual look that she suspected was copied from the latest men's fashion magazines. He had certainly come a long way from his trailer-park days. Susan noticed he had moved from his cubicle in the technology division into an office of his own.

"I'm afraid my hands are tied as far as influencing my brother goes. The best thing I could do for him was hire you as his attorney, and it seems he even managed to screw that up," Dorian said with a sad shake of his head. "I have to tell you that things around here are looking pretty grim. The police have impounded all of Sebastian's personal records."

A knock at the door put an abrupt halt to their conversation. The person on the other side of that door didn't bother waiting for an invitation to come in. A man who looked to be in his early thirties stepped inside and filled the small room with his presence. He introduced himself as Robert Cole.

Susan recognized the name immediately. "The private investigator Sebastian hired to look into the murder of Eric Chambers?" she asked.

"One and the same."

He was a particularly nice-looking man with clear blue eyes that gave the impression he could see right through you. Though she had the feeling Robert Cole knew exactly who she was, Susan introduced herself, anyway. Since he had been the one to uncover the threatening e-mail and was present when the fiscal records tying Sebastian to corporate embezzlement were discovered, she wondered if she wasn't, in fact, shaking hands with the enemy.

Dorian hastened to explain that they had already met at the Texas Cattleman's Club and asked him to sit down.

"What brings you here?" he asked pointedly.

"Just wrapping up a few loose ends on my investigation," Robert told them. "There's something unfinished about this case that's costing me sleep at night, and my wife is taking exception to it. She says I need all the beauty sleep I can get."

Susan was caught off guard by his easy manner. She could see why Seb had hired him. Beneath that handsome exterior was an intensity to finish the job he'd been hired to do. Susan was reassured by the fact that whatever was bothering him about this case wasn't going to be quelled with a paycheck alone.

Although Dorian looked startled when Robert took out a pen and a notebook and proceeded to ask him about his whereabouts on the night Eric Chambers was murdered, he did not appear worried that he might be implicated. He reached into his top desk drawer, took out a time-planner and quickly flipped to the date in question. He referred the investigator to the notations he had made for that day.

"I ate a late supper at the Royal Diner after a particularly trying day here at work," he explained. "I believe a waitress there by the name of Laura Edwards can vouch for that."

Robert Cole wrote the name down.

"Any possibility that you saw Sebastian Wescott that night?" he asked Dorian.

"Afraid not. I was under the belief that my half brother was out of town on business, but it seems that's a claim he's unable to substantiate."

"Anything else either of you would like to add while I've got you both here?" Robert asked.

Dorian thought for a moment before responding, "Just that I'm awfully worried about my brother. He's fired his attorney."

He gestured sympathetically toward Susan, who didn't bother to protest that she had quit the case voluntarily.

"Apparently he intends to represent himself in court," Dorian went on. "Not a particularly wise choice for a man with the kind of resources he has on hand. He looks like he hasn't slept for weeks, and I've smelled alcohol on his breath the past few times I've seen him. He's taking this pretty hard."

Dorian stopped to offer the investigator a piece of hard candy from a dish on his desk. He popped one into his own mouth and continued with wrinkled brow.

"If you have any influence on my brother at all, Robert, I'm begging you to encourage him not to jump bail. A lot of my friends have put up that money, and I'd hate to be the one to have to tell them that Sebastian let them down."

Susan was utterly shocked by the very idea. She opened her mouth to say so, but Robert got in the first word.

"Considering that the evidence I uncovered has put him in such a precarious position, I hardly think Sebastian Wescott would listen to anything I have to say. I'm not exactly high on his list of confidants right now. But I wouldn't be too worried about him skipping out on bail. He doesn't strike me as a particularly stupid man."

With that, Robert Cole excused himself and left just as suddenly as he had arrived. The mood in the wake of his exit was somber, to say the least. Susan watched hope slipping away like a helium balloon escaping reach as it soared out of sight, a bright red heart growing smaller and smaller against a dark-blue sky.

"Maybe he'll turn something up," Dorian offered in an encouraging voice.

"Maybe," she repeated dully.

Though neither of them sounded very hopeful, their only other choice was to give up in despair. Having used up all her tears for an entire lifetime, Susan was surprised to feel one slip down her cheek. Uncomfortable with such a womanly show of emotion, Dorian handed her a tissue from a box on his desk.

"Listen," he said, raking a hand through his hair in a way that reminded Susan of his half brother. That they were tied by blood was evident not only in their physical characteristics but also in some of their mannerisms. "I promise you that I'll have a word with Sebastian. I'll tell him how worried you are about him and do my best to persuade him to hire another lawyer to represent him. I've got to be honest with you, though. I really don't hold out much hope that I'll be able to change his mind."

In her heart, Susan didn't, either. Still, she appreciated Dorian's kindness to her and his obvious concern for Sebastian. She shouldn't underestimate the anguish that losing his half brother so soon after finding him was causing Dorian. She gave him a quick hug before leaving and hastened to get out of his office before she broke down completely. Short of making up an alibi for Sebastian and perjuring herself, Susan didn't know what more she could do to help the man she loved.

*   *   *

Sick at heart, she returned to her apartment, where she sank onto her couch without bothering to fix any dinner. She grabbed the remote and turned on the evening news. What she saw didn't do anything to lift her spirits. There, in living color, was Sebastian Wescott himself, caught in the glare of flashbulbs popping in his face. Reporters were shoving microphones at him, demanding to know, as he struggled to make his way down the front steps of the courthouse, whether rumors that he intended to represent himself were true. Susan didn't suppose he had considered the need to bring bodyguards with him to clear a path so that he could get to his vehicle.

"Mr. Wescott, can you tell us—"

"How will this affect Wescott Oil and all the people who work—"

"No comment."

Susan was relieved to see him stick to that phrase as the reporters persisted in badgering him and attempting to block his way.

"Did you murder Eric Chambers?" one yokel in back called out.

Susan held her breath as she waited to see if Sebastian was going to dive over the reporters in front and throttle the idiot who had asked the question.

"No, I did not," he replied, shoving a microphone out of his face.

"Hey!" the offended newsman hollered.

Though it was difficult to make any sense of the babble surrounding Sebastian's appearance, one question rang out loud and clear. It was a question that turned Sebastian's face six shades of furious.

"Is it true you fired Susan Wysocki as your attorney because the two of you had a lovers' spat? That you've separated because of irreconcilable differences?''

Susan cringed. She couldn't help but wonder if Joe himself hadn't somehow leaked that juicy bit of information to the press. Sebastian grabbed the nearest microphone and waited for silence before deeming to answer for the entire world to hear. Susan heard her own voice join the fray.

"No," she cried, fearing Sebastian was about to make a deal with the devil himself.

"For the record, I did not fire Ms. Wysocki. I would have been an idiot to do so. Susan Wysocki is one damned fine lawyer, the best I've ever had the good luck to run into. As much as I regret it, I have to respect her reasons for resigning from this case. I'd ask you to respect the woman's privacy and not subject her to the kind of abusive treatment that you clowns claim is the privilege of the press. In fact, I'd appreciate it if you'd just leave her name out of this altogether.''

The likelihood of that, now that Sebastian had so publicly stated his feelings on the matter, was next to nothing. In anticipation of the onslaught of incoming calls, Susan reached over and took her phone off the hook. She should have expected no less from a man who lived by his own unique code of honor and was willing to sacrifice himself if necessary to uphold it.

The close-up the cameraman took of Sebastian's face just before turning the incident over to the local anchor didn't do him justice. His features were too marked by torment to show how truly handsome he was. Susan was shocked to see that Dorian hadn't been exaggerating about his half brother's appearance. Telltale circles deepened his eyes, and in the harsh glare of the camera's light, his face took on a gaunt look.

It worried Susan to see the glint in the anchorman's eyes. The gray at his temples marked him as a veteran of the ratings wars. Clearly he saw this as his chance to make a name for himself in the big time and leave local coverage behind him. He had a hard time keeping the glee from his voice as Susan's name and face were flashed in a corner of the screen. He seemed to take perverse delight in the prospect of "bringing down" one of the most prosperous and respected men in the state. It was the kind of coup he had been waiting for his whole career.

Regardless of any personal pain inflicted on the injured parties themselves—not to mention the adverse effect it was sure to have on hundreds of people employed by Wescott Oil Enterprises—this fellow showed absolutely no compunction about taking advantage of others' misfortune. He might be the first to break the scoop, but Susan knew he would not be the last to exploit this story. That this time the target of the press was a millionaire would only amplify the carnival air of the coverage in the days to come. Too many people would silently gloat to see a rich man suffer simply because they were jealous of his success and would be quick to discount the hard work it took to achieve such wealth. It was a strange and twisted form of prejudice that would be hard to fight in court.

Moved by Sebastian's gallantry under fire in his

attempt to protect her, Susan didn't bothering asking herself why she had fallen in love with this obstinate, honorable man. Fighting it was useless. Without Sebastian, she was not whole. In the soft glow of the television tube, she simply came to accept this truth as one acknowledges that an arm or a leg is a part of one's self.

Just as she knew that she would wait an eternity for him if she must.

Eleven

Susan awoke on her rented sofa to find herself still dressed in the clothes she had worn to work the day before. She had neglected to turn off the television set before falling asleep, and the first thing she saw upon opening her eyes was the flickering image on her twenty-five-inch screen. It took a moment for her somnolent brain to recall last night's newscast, whereupon consciousness was upon her immediately. Pulling herself into a sitting position, she checked her watch and was glad to discover that it was far too early in the morning for even the most diehard reporters to begin pestering her.

Reaching for the phone on the floor beside her, she proceeded to put the receiver back on the hook. The first thing she intended to do after taking a refreshing shower, changing into more comfortable clothes and sipping a hot cup of flavored instant coffee was to place a call to Sebastian just as soon as the sun made an appearance in the eastern sky. She wondered if he was as eager to reconcile as she. Vowing to completely avoid the question about where he was on the night of the murder, she began framing arguments for why the two of them should get back together.

If that ultimately meant waiting until he was released from prison to begin their lives anew, so be it. Anticipating Sebastian's certain reluctance to tie her down to a man with a potential prison record, she constructed her case not on a logical premise but rather on the foundation of her own heart. Bars could not lock up the love she felt for this man. Nor could time diminish a passion that stemmed not from physical attraction alone but from an enduring respect for his intellectual and emotional strength.

However unstable the present might have been, Susan knew enough to let go of the past and grab hold of the present for all she was worth. Looking back over her life, she had never felt more imprisoned than when she had been married to Joe. Just because her relationship with him had been awful did not mean that Sebastian was not worthy of her trust. It was high time to separate then from now and to accept Seb's reasons for maintaining silence as honorable.

Susan was halfway to the bathroom when the phone rang. Not willing to take a chance on it being a nosy reporter, she decided to simply let the answering machine screen her calls. Still, she waited a moment before stepping out of the room on the off chance that it was Sebastian.

The woman's voice wafting softly into the room had the effect of exotic perfume upon her. It was utterly captivating.

"Ms. Wysocki," the woman said in a pleading tone that Susan doubted any man alive could find the strength to resist. "If you're there, Ms. Wysocki, please pick up the phone. I saw the newscast last night, and I think I can be of help. Sebastian Wescott was with me on the night in question. If it's the only way of securing his freedom, I would be willing to come forward and testify to the fact that he was no-where near the town of Royal, Texas, when that man Eric Chambers was murdered."

Susan sprung across the room with all the gusto of an Olympic sprinter and grabbed the phone. "Please don't hang up!" she implored, saying a si-lent prayer that she wasn't too late already.

The number on her caller-identity box flashed Not Available.

Silence greeted her directive.

"Hello, hello," she repeated breathlessly. "This is Susan Wysocki. Are you still there?"

Time was an endless string of beads stretching into eternity. The clock on the wall marked every single one of the seconds ticking by. Susan was just about to give up and write the whole thing off as a cruel hoax when a single, muted syllable gave her heart reason to leap with hope.

"Yes."

Sensing the caller's reluctance, Susan waited for her to continue without pressing too hard too soon.

Clearly this was a delicate matter, and the last thing she wanted to do was scare off the woman by being perceived as pushy.

"Can we meet someplace private?" Sebastian's self-confessed alibi asked hesitantly. "I don't trust phones—or lawyers, for that matter. It's only because Sebastian spoke so highly of you on the television that I'm willing to talk to you at all."

Susan detected a slight Spanish accent. The gentle quality of her voice was compelling and sensual at the same time. Susan desperately wanted to put a face to it.

"Name the time and the place, and I'll be there."

It was a challenge not to jump prematurely into the long pause that followed her offer. Clearly the woman to whom she was speaking had some deep reservations about coming forward.

"You have my word that I'll come alone," Susan volunteered when the silence became too much to bear. The breath froze in her lungs as she waited for a response.

"Is there any way my identity can be protected?"

Tinged with fear, that halting, mellifluous voice gave every impression that the wrong answer to this crucial question would terminate this conversation immediately. As critical as this testimony could be to freeing the man she loved, Susan did not want to obtain it under false pretenses. She answered as honestly as she could without compromising Sebastian's chance of an acquittal.

"I'm not sure. Once you explain your circumstances to me, I promise I'll do everything I can to accommodate you."

The sigh that met her promise seemed to transport this woman's soul through the telephone wires connecting them. Goose bumps raised the flesh on Susan's arms. Even without knowing any details, she felt a bond to this woman who held Sebastian's fate in her hands.

"The gazebo at Royalty Park. Midnight tonight."

With that, the line went dead.

Susan replaced the receiver with shaking hands. Clearly her anonymous caller wasn't taking any chances on being seen in public with Susan. It was a potentially dangerous rendezvous. Such a meeting could just as easily be a trap for Susan as a way to free Sebastian. Was she being set up, just as he claimed to have been?

One man was dead already. Murdered. There was no reason to believe that the killer would not strike again. Having been taught long ago that a woman should never venture into dark, out-of-the-way places alone at night, Susan couldn't keep violent visions from running through her head. She weighed the possibility of being knocked in the head, violated and killed against her love for Sebastian and the chance to preserve his reputation and his freedom.

There was no contest.

She would accept the risk. It was Sebastian's only chance.

Overjoyed at the prospect of actually being able to save the man she loved from public humiliation, financial ruin and prison time, Susan dismissed all thought of personal safety. All the same, she locked her door before venturing into the shower. She had a full head of lather worked up when an insidious thought occurred to her, causing her to reach out for the handrail to steady herself. The reason Sebastian refused to provide an alibi for the night in question was as painfully obvious as the soap in her eyes. He was protecting the mysterious woman on the phone. The caller's apprehensiveness about stepping into the public eye, as well as her request to keep her identity a secret, could be explained easily enough by any objective outside observer not blinded by love.

Sebastian was having an affair with a married woman.

And if the woman's husband was anything like Joe, Susan could well understand why she was afraid to reveal her secret. Certainly in the history of judicial annals, more than one jealous husband had been known to commit murder upon discovering his wife's infidelity. Had Eric Chambers somehow become mixed up in this whole sordid affair and taken the brunt of a spurned lover's uncontrollable rage? Or had he been foolish enough to try blackmailing his boss with the knowledge of his clandestine affair?

Sinking into a heap in the corner of the shower, Susan let the hot water slowly turn to cold. Her tears were washed down the drain as the impact of Sebastian's betrayal stabbed her like thousands of tiny knives. The only logical reason he would continue to protect this woman in the face of a possible life sentence was that he was in love with her. That in itself was more devastating to Susan than the fact that he had conducted an affair with a married woman.

She felt her stomach heave. All the while he had been making passionate love to her, he had likely been imagining another woman in his bed. The

thought made her feel dirty, and no amount of scrub-
bing could ever make her feel clean again.

To think she had believed him to be a man of
principle! How devastating to realize that the greater
cause to which Sebastian was so willing to sacrifice
himself was, in fact, another woman. The only reason
Susan could think of that he would refuse to implicate her was that she was married and he felt bound
to protect her honor. The case that was once certain
to win Susan acclaim and secure her firm's success
had now broken her heart and destroyed her faith in
the man she loved.

What a fool she was! To be duped twice in one
lifetime into falling for a man of bad character didn't
speak very highly of her own. Sadly Susan dragged
herself out of the shower and wrapped a towel
around her body, then spent the next hour with the
lights off, staring into the darkness and probing her
open wounds.

Anger came along to numb the pain.

How dare the birds outside her window chirp such
a cheerful welcome to the sun when it rose only to
shine light on her lover's indiscretions? Revenge was
tempting. It would serve Sebastian Wescott right if
she spent the whole night flirting her eyeballs out at
some singles bar, all the while letting his mystery
lady turn blue in the cold waiting for her to show up.
There was no earthly reason she shouldn't let him
rot in jail for the next three decades. Maybe she
should give that cocky anchorman down at Channel
One the opportunity to film her slapping a hypocrite
in public.

Before she did anything, however, Susan decided

it was only fair to give Sebastian an opportunity to explain himself. Memory directed her fingers as she dialed his home phone number. Any action, she decided, was preferable to wallowing in the pit of self-pity.

"Is something wrong?" Rosa asked, obviously worried by the anger she detected in Susan's voice.

Susan did her best to keep her suspicions to herself. As devoted as Rosa was to Sebastian, there was always the possibility that she would blame his behavior on his father's bad genes. It was not a theory to which Susan personally subscribed. Having worked with her fair share of criminals eager to attribute their misdeeds to genetic flaws and difficult childhoods, she believed that a man was responsible for his own actions.

She was disappointed to hear that Sebastian had just left for a meeting at the Texas Cattleman's Club. For all she knew, he was down there right now sharing a big laugh at her expense with all his buddies. The thought made her furious enough to actually consider marching right down there and breaking down the doors of that archaic establishment, if necessary, to confront him face-to-face.

The doorman dryly told her to "take a number" as he directed Susan to the "ladies' parlor" and suggested she make herself comfortable. Apparently the club members were in a very important meeting and had left word with him that they were not to be disturbed. Determined to wait however long it took, even if it meant planting herself there like the potted orchid in one corner of the room, Susan took a seat on a newly reupholstered blue velvet settee that dated back to the turn of the century. Instead of the heavy paneling she had spied in the main room, these walls were covered with a delicate rose print that somehow made her feel out of place in her cream-colored slacks and pale-green sleeveless shell. Such a room called for long white gloves, extravagant hats and dresses trimmed with lace.

All things considered, the atmosphere was cozy enough, even if did smack of old-fashioned chauvinism dating back to the days when men banished women from their presence so they could smoke cigars and speak of matters too weighty for their wives to trouble their pretty little heads over. Indeed, the potpourri simmering in an electrical pot on the marble-top table next to Susan failed to completely mask the odor of a hundred years' worth of such cigars enjoyed on the premises. In the middle of the room, an authentic Royal Bayreuth tea service was displayed atop a cherry stand polished to a gleam. At the moment Susan would have preferred something more substantial in the way of beverages. Even though the club seldom received unannounced female visitors outside the usual charity ball or community shindig, she suspected the tea was nonetheless kept piping hot. Impatient with such pretty folderol, Susan felt like hurling the whole set against one of the many gilded mirrors decorating all four walls.

"Ridiculous, isn't it?" asked a distinctly feminine voice from across the room. "Keeping us waiting here in a holding tank deemed the ladies' parlor as if women are some kind of alien invaders out to destroy their safe haven rather than acknowledging the fact that we do make up at least half the population of this planet.''

The woman who stepped out from behind a tall philodendron beneath a veiled cornice wore an expression of disgust similar to Susan's. The only difference being, this fiery redhead looked as if she would just as soon grab an antique gun off the wall in the hallway outside as stoop to smashing china as a way of expressing her outrage.

Crossing the room in quick strides, she stuck out her hand and introduced herself simply enough as Meredith Silver. A petite five feet in height, she would have little trouble crawling through the air duct that she had been studying before she introduced herself. Susan was immediately struck by the energy the young woman radiated. All her features were animated, but her eyes were particularly expressive. The storm brewing in those arresting gray orbs did not bode well for whoever might happen to get in the way of this human tornado.

The warmth of Meredith's handshake belied the indignation of her words. Susan felt an instant bond of sisterhood not entirely explained by the fact that they were thrown together by such unusual circumstances.

''Susan Wysocki,'' she introduced herself.

Relieved to be spared the torture of searching for anything more interesting than the latest in diet advice in the stack of glossy ladies' magazines provided, Susan attempted to keep her own emotions in check by carrying on polite conversation with Meredith. It couldn't help but make the time pass more quickly.

"How long do you think it'll be?" Susan asked, checking her watch for at least the tenth time since she had arrived at the front door.

"Before they come out or I go in after him?" Meredith asked.

Her response coaxed a smile from Susan, although she wasn't so sure that it was meant to be tongue-in-cheek.

"Which 'him' are you referring to?" she wanted to know. It occurred to her that she had perhaps stumbled upon yet another in a long line of Sebastian's conquests.

"Dorian Brady."

Meredith spat the name out. "I'm here to see that that good-for-nothing, low-down skunk pays for what he did to my sister."

She gestured emphatically to make her point, causing her long auburn curls to bounce with fury. The glow of the Tiffany light fixture overhead emphasized red highlights that matched her temper. Susan thought camouflage gear would have suited this little spitfire far better than the pink sweater and matching slacks she was wearing.

As stunned by the ferocity in that open declaration of war as she was by the fact that Meredith named Dorian as the cad in question, Susan could only assume he had done something dastardly, like getting some poor girl pregnant and running out on her. Meredith's loyalty touched a chord deep inside her. Susan wished there was some way of showing her empathy. Thinking of how she herself would react if her little sister was poorly used, she shook her head in disgust.

"Dirty deeds must run in the family," she muttered. "I'm here to confront his half brother."

This bit of information served to further galvanize Meredith's resolve to take action. Fury blazed in her eyes. Seeing as she had already divulged more than she had probably intended, Meredith was clearly impatient to make a move. Instead, she made a bold announcement.

"I'm going in."

Susan was reminded of a Green Beret single-handedly launching an attack on an enemy position. It sounded like a suicide mission to her.

"Are you sure that's wise?" she asked, knowing it would take more than pluck alone to storm such a fortress.

As if to forestall Susan from trying to talk her out of it, Meredith mumbled, "Cover my back," as she darted out the door and down the corridor. Susan was tempted to call "Remember the Alamo" after her, but didn't much care for the images the saying evoked. She had little time to gather her thoughts before the sound of rioting broke out. The thought of one tiny gal taking on the whole of the Texas Cattleman's Club by herself made Susan laugh. It was a sound she thought she would never hear again.

She wished she were more like the spirited Meredith Silver, who would let nothing stand in the way of retribution. Though Susan doubted whether the younger woman would attempt anything more serious than shaking up this archaic gentleman's club by attempting to publicly shame Dorian, she had to admire Meredith's grit. From the sounds of it, she was holding her own in there. Susan wondered just how many men it would actually take to remove her from the premises.

Unfortunately she could ill afford to let her desire to join Meredith in the fray get in the way of what she knew she must do. In any case, Susan knew there was little point in trying to contact Sebastian in the midst of such a melee. Just as she suddenly knew that nothing he had to say would dissuade her from going to Royalty Park at midnight to meet the mystery woman who owned his heart. For while his heart was traitorous, hers was not.

As much as Susan could not bear the thought of him spending the rest of his life with another woman, she could not allow vengeance to supplant justice. If it could be proved that Sebastian was, in fact, with someone else on the night Eric Chambers was killed, she would set aside her personal feelings and do everything in her power to bring that information to light. Though rage was certain to keep alive the sense of betrayal she felt at Sebastian's hands, even now it could not erase the memory of the breathtaking heights to which he had taken her. Susan could not bring herself to regret giving herself over to Sebastian so completely. He had taught her how to love again, and that in itself was no small matter.

Truth was, even such acute pain was better than the numbness with which she had been living before Sebastian had blown her safe little world all apart. She had escaped the cage Joe had built for her only to incarcerate herself behind bars forged with the paralyzing fear of ever again entrusting her heart to another. With his words and actions Joe had done his best to convince her that she was nothing without him. But his love had been too small to hold her.

Sebastian erred in the opposite extreme. Perhaps it was his jet-setting background and his father's poor example that led him to believe he could love two women at the same time.

Her heart was not so generous. The love she felt for Sebastian was all-consuming. She could not share *her* heart with another. Not now. Not ever. She simply wasn't made that way.

Just as she could never forget the times they spent together, she could never forgive him for what he had done to her. Whatever they had together was over.

However, that did not mean she could shut off her feelings for him like a spigot. She still loved him. Fool that she was, Susan suspected she always would. Her aching heart would not let her believe otherwise. But she was not so vindictive that she would knowingly let an innocent man go to prison just to keep him from the arms of another woman.

Meredith Silver's voice could be heard echoing throughout the building as Susan slipped unnoticed out the front door of the venerable Texas Cattleman's Club to lay her life on the line for Sebastian Wescott, the man she believed had betrayed her love.

Twelve

Sebastian was not the only one shocked to see Susan at his preliminary hearing. He supposed that the fact that he hadn't bothered hiring another attorney had something to do with her presence in the courtroom today. As grateful as he was for the last-minute show of support, he didn't want her to mistake his refusal to replace her as some grandiose gesture or play for pity. It wasn't. The truth was, he simply found her irreplaceable.

Ever since she had moved out, Sebastian could think of little else but how desperately he missed her. Having never been "lovesick" before, he had a horrible new appreciation of the medical connotation associated with this disease. Lethargy, loss of appetite, irritability, headaches and insomnia were just some of the symptoms he had had the past week. In the grip of this debilitating malady, he came to understand the darker side of passion. Facing a possible life term in prison wasn't any more wretched than facing life without Susan's love and support.

Her being here meant more to him than she would ever understand. Sebastian wanted to believe that it signified not only that she knew him to be incapable of committing such a heinous crime, but that she had come to respect, if not completely understand, his motives for keeping his alibi secret.

The crisp, powder-blue suit Susan wore underscored her femininity without compromising her professionalism. Acting as if she was oblivious to the stir she caused simply by walking into the room unannounced, Susan looked as determined as Sebastian had ever seen her. Indeed, only someone very brave or very stupid would dare to try to stop this high-heeled warrior as she purposefully strode down the aisle.

Looking straight ahead at the judge, she deliberately avoided eye contact with Sebastian.

He couldn't have taken his eyes off her had he been ordered by the judge to do so. With her blond hair pulled up and away from her face, he could see signs of the stress of the past few days. Her naturally pale complexion appeared wan, and dark circles emphasized the anguish in her eyes. She asked for permission to approach the bench. In light of their ugly breakup, he would have to assume that seeing her again under harsh fluorescent lighting and in such strained conditions would lessen any romantic feelings he had for her.

Quite the contrary, he longed to loosen that golden

cascade of hair from its constraining bun as he was hit broadside by a flashback of that silken mass splayed out on his pillow. His need to reach out and touch her lodged itself as a physical ache dead center in his chest. Right where his heart used to be, before he'd lost it to her.

Sebastian felt a cold draft when she breezed past him as if he were invisible. He was confused by her failure to acknowledge him. Confused, and deeply hurt. Why would she bother showing up at all if she couldn't spare him so much as a passing glance? If she wasn't here to support him, just exactly what was she up to?

Aside from the fact that he didn't much care for the idea of plea-bargaining when he hadn't committed any crime, Sebastian doubted whether the prosecutor would agree to reduce the charge, anyway. The influence of intensive public opinion, media saturation, political pressures and Seb's own refusal to negotiate made that a highly unlikely possibility. He certainly hoped Susan wasn't here to beg him for a last-minute explanation of where he was on the night of the murder. They had covered that territory before, and it had gotten them nowhere but lost and estranged from one another. As tempting as it was to save his own skin, Sebastian had two innocent lives, as well as the sacred trust of the Texas Cattleman's Club to consider. A man who was governed by his own code of honor, he simply put his trust in God and prayed that justice would prevail.

Perhaps she was going to enter a plea of insanity on his behalf?

"This is highly irregular," cried the district attorney.

Mr. McCallaster had thinning blond hair and an ambitious wife who frequently badgered him to do whatever it took to advance his career beyond the paltry earning potential of a public servant. A murder case of this magnitude was the perfect vehicle for obtaining the public exposure necessary to catapult them into a bigger house. Undoubtedly it would have a pool in back and an impressive address that declared their upward mobility to the entire world— and specifically to a father-in-law who thought his little girl could have done a heck of a lot better for herself.

"I was given to understand that Ms. Wysocki had taken herself off this case," Mr. McCallaster protested.

Judge Walters seemed to be listening sympathetically to the prosecution. He wasn't one to tolerate any shenanigans in his courtroom. He had been quoted as saying that the press could expect the same kind of access to the case of a millionaire accused of murder that he allowed for anyone else who came before him—which was next to nothing. As far as this grizzled old judge was concerned, the press corps could line up like vultures on a fence post outside the courtroom, but as long as he was in charge, the proceedings were closed to the media. Feeling the beat of their wings as the scavengers flocked around this preliminary hearing, he could only imagine what kind of a circus they would turn a full-fledged trial into.

The brass spittoon beside his bench rang out with

an all-too-visual expression of his opinion of the media in general. His aim was impeccable. As was the way this old country boy intended to run a court of law.

"Calm down, Norm, and try to remember we're not at the trial stage yet," he said with a weariness that had permanently settled into the lines of his brow.

The judge hoped it wasn't necessary to explain to the prosecutor that he need only present enough evidence to convince the court that a crime had been committed and that there was "reasonable and probable cause" to believe that Sebastian Wescott had perpetrated it. Although this was not as stringent a standard as proving someone guilty beyond a "reasonable doubt," as required at the trial stage, it did prevent the kind of tyrannical abuses that historically occurred when the English Crown enjoyed the right of initiating criminal prosecutions.

"I suggest you save the theatrics for a jury, if things progress that far."

Having spent the better part of the last month salivating over this case, the prosecutor paled at the possibility of a dismissal. The judge nodded at Susan and gestured for her to come forward. She expressed whatever it was she had come to impart so quietly that the old man had to lean forward a little in his seat to hear her. His weathered face gave away nothing, but a moment later he motioned for the prosecutor to come forward, as well.

Still frowning, Mr. McCallaster vehemently shook his head as the judge rose from his seat and led both Susan and him out the side door. He knew better than to open his mouth again, however. There was too much at stake here to alienate the judge before they even reached the point of jury selection.

No one said a word to either Sebastian or the prosecutor's special assistant, a stocky young man who wore a badly cut suit and cheap tie much like the pair of glasses perched on his nose—a little askew. He began riffling through his briefcase for no apparent reason other than to cover his own confusion and embarrassment at being so visibly left out of the loop. Aside from the bailiff, they were the only two left in the room.

The quiet was broken only by the dull hum of an overhead ceiling fan that did little but move the warm air around the room. Sunlight spilled in through high windows where the gardener waged a weekly war to keep the ivy in check. It crawled up the walls of the old brick edifice, lending an air of charm to the outside courtyard area. By contrast, the interior was stark and drab. The institutional beige carpet beneath Sebastian's feet was worn, and the chair he sat on was wooden and uncomfortable. Scars on the armrests gave the impression that more than one defendant had clawed at the wood with bare fingernails while awaiting a verdict.

Sebastian was tempted to tug at his tie and fling it across the room. He felt as if he was suffocating. April was nearly over, and the air-conditioning had yet to be turned on. Beneath a conservative dark suit jacket, his pristine white shirt was growing damp with perspiration. An impatient man by nature, he had been on jungle missions that were less stressful than sitting here in ignorance waiting. And waiting. And waiting....

The woman waiting for the judge in his private quarters was even more beautiful than Susan had first observed. Not even the moon had cooperated that night at the gazebo the first and only time that they had met. Dark clouds had obstructed its glow as effectively as the veil the mystery woman had needlessly worn to cover her face. Susan had secretly hoped that the sultry voice that had so reluctantly agreed to come forward emanated from a less-attractive body.

Up until now she hadn't so much as divulged her name. When Susan had pressed her for information, she had jumped up from her seat as if to bolt. Realizing her mistake, Susan was quick to relent. Seeing how this woman's testimony was the only thing standing between Sebastian and a prison term, she could hardly afford to indulge her own gloomy curiosity. Clothed all in black, the mysterious woman had deliberately chosen to blend in with the shadows of the night. She had looked over her shoulder often. Small noises frightened her: the wind rattling the chains of the playground swings, a squirrel jumping from branch to branch, an owl asking the same question Susan longed to ask: Who? Who? Just who exactly are you?

Their clandestine encounter had lasted no more than five minutes, only long enough for Susan to procure an assurance that the woman would indeed consent to speak to the judge in his chambers. Alone. Under the circumstances, Susan was hesitant to make such a promise. Not only did she doubt the judge's willingness to agree to such an outrageous demand, she wasn't completely convinced the woman herself would show. She certainly didn't relish the thought of making a fool of herself in front of a judge she respected.

More than once since that night, Susan wondered if she had dreamed the encounter. Relief showed on her face when the judge opened the door to his chambers and she saw that the room was not empty. He wasted no time in bidding both the district attorney and Susan to enter.

"I thought I stipulated that I would talk only to the judge. Who is this man?"

The woman asking the question pointed to the only other man in the room. Fear was tangible in the air as she cowered in her chair, reminding Susan of a cornered kitten. Unsheathing her claws, she did everything but hiss her displeasure at being thus betrayed. For a moment Susan feared she would attempt to dart around them and make an escape without divulging what she had come to say.

"This is the prosecuting attorney, Norman McCallaster," Judge Walters said without further ado. "I asked him to be here. He has to be privy to this conversation if I'm going to be persuaded to dismiss this case based on what you have to tell me."

Temporarily satisfied that Norm wasn't some thug hired to abduct her, the woman settled back into her chair. "Can you give me any assurance that what I have to say will be held confidential?"

"Young woman," the judge responded with a sigh that underscored his growing annoyance, "you are sorely testing my patience. I agreed to this meeting on your terms. What you have to say will determine what I'll do from here.''

Susan couldn't blame Sebastian for falling in love with such a rare beauty. She had bright blue eyes the color of untroubled skies, thick black hair cascading down to the middle of her back and alabaster skin that Snow White would have envied. Her shapely figure was sheathed in a soft cashmere dress that was as classy as the rest of her. Even her gestures seemed refined as she folded her hands on her lap and struck a ladylike pose. All she was missing to present the image of a perfect Southern belle was a hoop skirt and a delicate drawl. The woman seemed to Susan to be loveliness personified.

She did not, however, strike her as the type of woman who would indulge in an indiscriminate affair.

''My name is Rachael Gilberte,'' she said softly. ''And I can vouch for Sebastian Wescott's being with me at the time Eric Chambers was murdered.''

Again Susan was struck by the subtlest hint of a Spanish accent lacing that soft, cultured voice.

''Are you romantically involved with Mr. Wescott?'' the judge asked pointedly.

It was the question Susan had been longing to ask herself, but had been too afraid to hear the answer. Not only would it taint the woman's testimony and render it suspect, it was also certain to wreak havoc with Susan's own ability to remain standing. She braced herself against a nearby wall and crossed her arms over her chest, hoping to keep herself from falling apart on the spot.

Rachael's face reflected genuine astonishment at the question.

"Is that what you think?" she asked with a shake of her head. "I assure you that I didn't come here today out of any romantic notion, but rather out of a sense of loyalty and appreciation to the bravest, most selfless man I know."

Her ensuing tale was as fantastic as any Susan had ever heard.

And far more compelling.

Rachael Gilberte claimed that she had been both young and naive when she married an older man of considerable means, believing him to be a respectable businessman. It had taken her some time to realize that the bulk of his wealth could be attributed to his participation in an international drug cartel, which he refused to acknowledge in her company. Although marriage quickly revealed Tomás to be both a controlling and ruthless man, she had not thought him capable of cold-blooded murder. Had she not witnessed her husband gun down a rival in their holiday villa, Rachael would never have believed it herself. Luckily her presence had gone undetected.

Paralyzed with fear, she waited several days before approaching him to ask for a divorce, citing irreconcilable differences that included at least one mistress that she knew of. Tomás had laughed at the boldness of her request and then beat her severely. The next morning she found a single suitcase packed and sitting on the marble front steps. A musclebound "chauffeur" delivered her to the airport with a one-way ticket and orders never to return. It was an edict she would have been grateful to obey had it not been for one very significant deterrent.

Her son.

David was but four years old when his mother had been exiled from his life. Iron gates and armed gunmen held him captive on his father's estate, from which no amount of legal maneuvering could free him. The Mexican government appeared indifferent to the pleas of an American woman they claimed had willfully abandoned her husband and child. Aside from the fact that Tomás was so masterful at greasing the right palms, officials argued they had too much to do to in upholding the civil liberties of their own citizens, let alone some affluent divorcée living in comfort across the border.

Encumbered by international laws, the American judicial system was unable to do what Sebastian Wescott had. Rachael was at the point of abandoning all hope when he had arrived on her doorstep like a guardian angel sent from on high. How he knew of her desperate situation was of little concern to her, although she suspected a mutual friend and member, like Sebastian, of the Texas Cattleman's Club of intervening on her behalf. In any case, rather than questioning Sebastian's motives, she embraced the hope he offered her.

"He sneaked past the guards and into Tomás's very home to rescue my son at great personal risk and return him to me."

"Do you expect us to believe such a farfetched story?" Norman blurted at the conclusion of her remarks.

Norman's bluster didn't fool Susan any. She knew

a jury was certain to be moved by such an incredible tale of woe and felt sympathy for the woman who told it. God knew, she was. As much as Norm would hate putting such a compelling and beautiful witness on the stand, Susan suspected he wouldn't willingly forgo the chance of a lifetime, either. Not unless Rachael could come up with an ironclad alibi for Sebastian.

"Indeed I do," Rachael Gilberte said calmly. "I brought along an eyewitness to back me up."

Thirteen

Feeling as if she expected an armed guerrilla to charge out and take them all hostage, Susan jumped back in alarm when the closet door swung open. A little boy no bigger than the set of golf clubs that the judge kept beneath his coat in that very closet stepped into the room, blinking his eyes at the bright light. It was not at all what Susan had anticipated.

She was embarrassed by the sigh of relief that escaped her lips. One glance at this beautiful dark-haired boy indicated that Sebastian was not his biological father. The possibility that he and Rachael had created a child together was something that Susan had, in fact, considered over the past few tortured days. With eyes as black as ripe olives, the boy's features were identical to the man in the picture that Rachael had presented to the group. He smiled hesitantly, his teeth flashing white.

"Judge Walters, this is my son, David."

"I'm seven," he said proudly, while the adults in the room silently calculated the three long years he had been separated from his mother.

Without prompting, he offered the judge a manly handshake that tugged at the heart of every adult in the room. The pride in Rachael's voice was mirrored in her eyes as the sacred bond between a mother and child was immortalized in the moment. Watching Rachael lovingly push a lock of black hair away from his forehead, Susan felt her eyes sting. Once upon a time, lying in Sebastian's arms, she had foolishly allowed her imagination to conjure up a child conceived of their mutual love.

The prosecutor's brusque question intruded on Susan's memories. "What did Sebastian Wescott expect from you in return for his alleged heroics?" he demanded to know.

The question evoked a strong response from Rachael. Her disgust at Norman's implication was evident in her lovely features.

"Who questions the altruism of an angel when you are standing inside the gates of hell? Although I offered to pay him everything I own, which is little enough, he refused to take so much as a dime from me. Not for the rescue attempt itself. Nor for his part in establishing a new identity and home for my son and me."

This bit of information had the impact of a baseball bat directed squarely at Susan's forehead. Everything became clear to her. No wonder Sebastian felt honor bound to take his alibi to the grave with him! When he had said that two innocent lives were at stake, he wasn't exaggerating.

"It is for this reason that I ask you to please keep my identity a secret," Rachael implored.

Making eye contact with each and every person in the room, she proceeded to cover her son's ears and speak so softly that he could not overhear.

"I assure you Tomás would stop at nothing to get David back, and that includes killing me and anyone else who dares to get in his way."

Judge Walters rubbed his white goatee in contemplation as he assessed this woman's request.

"If the three of you wouldn't mind stepping out into the hallway for a moment, I want to speak to David alone," he said.

An expert at sniffing out the truth, he felt certain that he would be able to ascertain whether the child had been coached. Making note of the mother's worried expression, he hastened to assure her, "I don't intend to traumatize the boy, just to verify the details of such an amazing story without your presence in the room. I want to give David the opportunity to speak freely."

If Rachael feared a trap, she did her best to hide it as she bent down and deposited a kiss on her son's cheek. "There's nothing to be afraid of, honey," she promised. "I'll be right outside that door. You can call out if you need me. Just tell the judge the truth, and then we can go on home."

Home.

The word was a fragrant blossom lingering in the air. Susan couldn't imagine what it would be like to try raising a child on the run without a place to call

home. To live in fear of someone kidnapping your
son. Having to abandon your own identity in hopes
of creating a normal life for a child who has seen too
much in so few years…

Tomás would haunt both mother and child forever.
That Sebastian had remained silent to protect their
identity and keep their whereabouts a secret from
such a monster only made him all the more honorable to Susan. She berated herself for making the
unforgivable mistake of failing to take him at his
word.

She would just as soon go to jail herself as endanger this fragile family by incurring the kind of pub-
licity guaranteed to surround their testimony if this
case were to actually go to court. Indeed, Rachael's
impending demise would make for a stunning TV
movie-of-the-week. The international outrage alone
was enough to make a pack of hungry journalists
smack their lips over a possible Pulitzer for the story.
Each minute that ticked by as they waited in the hallway for the judge's decision seemed a year long.

Feeling a gentle hand on her shoulder, Susan was
surprised to see Rachael offering *her* comfort rather
than the other way around. The woman's words were
balm to Susan's spirit.

"I appreciate what you have done for me, Ms.
Wysocki. You promised to do your best to keep my
secret, and I believe you have. In any case, I owe
Sebastian so very much. There is no sacrifice I could
make that could ever compare to what he risked on
my account. If the judge dismisses my testimony as
farfetched, I don't want you to blame yourself. Come

what may, I would never stand by and allow such a man to be convicted on my account.''

Susan was spared trying to respond through a blur of tears by David's abrupt appearance. It was the second time in less than an hour that the simple act of his opening a door made her body flood with adrenaline. He was holding a lollipop in one hand and grinning.

''The judge wants to see both of us together, Mami.''

Rachael removed her hand from Susan's shoulder to square her own. As she was straightening her dark skirt, her son slipped a sticky hand into Susan's.

''You're pretty,'' he told her.

Falling into those beautiful dark eyes of his, Susan wondered how his mother had ever found the courage to come forward. Like Sebastian, she had her doubts about asking a woman to jeopardize the safety of her offspring. She couldn't imagine what it would be like to be tossed on the horns of such a dilemma.

Before stepping back into the judge's quarters, David asked an unexpected favor of her. ''Would you give this to Mr. Sebastian for me?''

The paper that he handed her had been folded many times and showed the wear of overhandling. It was just the right size to slip into the pocket of her suit jacket.

''I'd be honored,'' Susan told him solemnly.

She had to fight the urge to pull this cherub to her breast and hold him tight. His innocence stirred in her an instinct of motherly protection.

As the door clicked shut behind Rachael and David, she heard the prosecutor swear under his breath.

Although she couldn't be sure the judge would move
for dismissal, her gut told her that anyone would
have to be made out of marble not to be moved by
this boy's plight. Right, wrong or otherwise, she
could not refrain from taking a peek at the commu-
niqué David had given her. She was very careful
about unfolding it. Having every intention of deliv-
ering this message herself, she didn't want so much
as a single wrinkle to give away the fact that she had
viewed this prior to giving it to Sebastian. She
couldn't help wondering if it wasn't a letter from
Rachael herself and whether she had misrepresented
any romantic connection between them.

Opening the yellow sheet of drawing paper as if
it was an ancient manuscript of great historic value,
Susan gasped at what she saw. Depicted in a childish
drawing was Sebastian wearing a pair of angel wings
and holding a youngster in his arms. They were flying through a barrage of bullets coming from machine guns pointed at them from the bottom of the
page. Off to the side was a dark-haired, blue-eyed
mother holding her arms open to her child. At the
top of the sheet of paper was a simple inscription
written in a crude, childish script: "Thank you for
saving my life."

Tears filled Susan's eyes. A sob rose to her lips.
Never one to cry in public, she knew nothing could
stop those tears from falling freely down her face.
They spattered all over the drawing, ruining any
chance she might have had to plead innocent to a
charge of tampering with Sebastian's mail. That was
of little consequence at the moment. Right now she
was too busy rebuking herself for doubting him. That

she had actually thought him capable of carrying on with another woman when avowing his love for her made Susan feel very small and dirty-minded.

More ashamed than relieved, she wouldn't blame him for turning his back on her altogether.

"I'll be go to hell," she heard Norman mutter over her shoulder. "It's true, then."

Perhaps Susan should have taken more care to keep the prosecutor from taking a peek at David's drawing, but she couldn't bring herself to regret it. Everybody knew that Sebastian Wescott had been implicated in a murder. Very few would ever know what a hero he really was. That such a man had suffered the indignity of being fingerprinted and smeared in the press based on circumstantial evidence that had obviously been planted with the intention of framing him was unthinkable. That the real murderer was still at large was a worrying thought.

With his plan to put Sebastian behind bars thwarted, who knew what the killer would do next?

Susan managed a shaky smile as she turned to her colleague.

"Look on the bright side, Norm," she told him in an encouraging voice. "You still have a murder case to prosecute. All you've got to do now is find the right suspect."

Ambition notwithstanding, Norman McCallaster was a fair man. He no more wanted to put Rachael and her son in danger than he wanted to put an innocent man in prison. Though aspiring, he was neither malicious nor unethical. He told both the judge and Susan as much when they were called back into chambers. The judge, the prosecutor and Susan all vowed in one another's presence that what occurred in this closed chamber would forever remain secreted in their respective hearts.

When Susan reentered the courtroom with the prosecutor and proceeded to follow him to his designated table across the room, Sebastian felt his heart drop out beneath him. Standing there side by side, it appeared they had joined forces. That she still refused to look at him didn't bode well for his cause. As much as it tore him apart, he couldn't think badly of her for teaming up with the highly regarded Mr. McCallaster. By refusing to confide to her his alibi, he hadn't left her much choice in the matter. She could either watch her own business go under with his own while waiting for him to be released from prison or go on with her life without him.

The judge entered the room and took his seat. He looked at his watch as if surprised by how much time had elapsed. Unlike Susan, he had no problem fixing his gaze upon the defendant. Red, watery eyes bore into Sebastian and held him to his seat as effectively as any pair of handcuffs. He cleared his throat before speaking in a voice that, despite its age, resonated with absolute authority throughout the courtroom.

"Recent evidence presented to the court has cast reasonable doubt on the probability that the defendant was involved in the murder of Eric Chambers. Therefore, this court has decided that there is not probable cause to believe Sebastian Wescott perpetrated the crime of which he is accused. Case dismissed."

With that, the black-robed old gentleman rose

from his seat and left the courtroom. Not that Sebastian expected an apology from the court or from the prosecutor. Had there been any spectators present, Sebastian imagined they would have raised the rafters with their exclamations of surprise at this unexpected bolt from the bench. He was glad that no reporters were at hand to capture the astonishment on his own face. Relief sagged his shoulders as he threw his head back and exhaled deeply.

He could not believe it was over. It was anticlimactic, to say the least, but he was not about to complain. His life was his own again. Sebastian knew only one person with the fortitude, the brains and the moxie to manage such an incredible turn of events. He only hoped Susan hadn't endangered anyone in the process.

He watched her shake hands with Norman McCallaster and smile into the perplexed face of the assistant prosecutor. If the poor man was expecting some kind of explanation, neither Susan nor his boss appeared willing to give him one. He was still sputtering in disbelief when Norman escorted him out of the room and Sebastian found himself alone with Susan.

The distance separating them was as wide as the ocean. And as inconsequential as the thin air holding them apart. Susan smiled. Neither spoke. Rather, they cherished the moment for what it was: the possibility of a new beginning.

Sebastian was the first to pierce the silence.

"How did you manage it?" he asked.

Susan came away from the sidebar to stand before him. It was all she could do to keep from throwing herself into his arms and begging for his forgiveness. Handing David's drawing over to him, she confronted him with the evidence of his incredible act of courage. He stood there a long time looking at the crude rendering. When he spoke again, his voice was clogged with emotion.

"I didn't want them involved."

Reading the censure in his expression, Susan tried to allay his worries.

"Rachael came forward on her own. As much as she appreciated your selfless gesture, she didn't want you to go to prison on her account. Luckily the judge agreed. He also agreed to keep her testimony and her identity confidential."

"And what about the prosecutor?" Sebastian asked.

Now that Susan understood his sense of protectiveness toward Rachael did not stem from any romantic involvement, she loved him all the more for his concern for the mother and child who had entered and left her life shrouded in mystery. Undoubtedly a man with such strong instincts would make a wonderful father.

"Norman can be trusted," she assured him. "Besides, neither he nor I know where Rachael and her little boy are off to. Her secret is safe, Sebastian. And so are you—for the time being, that is."

The fact that the judge had exonerated him didn't mean that whoever had gone to such lengths to implicate him in a murder was going to let it go at that. Susan felt a shiver run through her at the thought, but Sebastian didn't allow her to dwell on it for long.

"How can I ever repay you for what you have done for me?" he asked.

She had given him his life back, but he had to wonder what it was worth without her in it.

Susan felt as rebuffed as if he had opened his wallet and offered to pay her off in hundred-dollar increments. His manner was so stiff that she worried that he did not intend to forgive her. Not that she could blame him. How often had he told her that his word should be more than enough if she truly loved him? It appeared that her lack of trust had cost her the love of a lifetime.

Still, that didn't mean she couldn't rise above her own grief and offer him the apology he was due. He was a man who hated to be in anyone's debt, so she gave him an answer that was intended to assuage his wounded pride and absolve Susan.

"You could start by forgiving me for ever doubting you."

Her voice cracked, and she struggled to remain standing on gelatinous knees. Sebastian reached out for her. His touch burned through layers of clothing like a brand. Helpless, she fell against him.

Strong arms encircled her and kept her upright. Tipping up her chin, he forced her to look into his eyes. She could see his very soul glimmering in the depths of those matching silver moons. It was pure and honest and good through and through.

"I'm the one who owes you an apology, Counselor," he said with a smile. "Having entrusted you with my heart, I should have trusted you with my secret. I'm sorry, Susan. So very sorry for the pain I caused you."

For the second time in less than an hour, Susan began to sob. Her tears made dark spots on his suit jacket and soaked through to his heart.

"Don't cry, sweetheart," he begged. "Not while I'm trying to propose to you."

Susan looked up at him in disbelief. Smiling, he nodded his head in affirmation and got down on bended knee before continuing.

"I have never been as lonely or incomplete as when you left me. Under the circumstances, I didn't feel I had the right to ask you to consider me for anything other than a prison pen pal. Now that you have worked a miracle in my defense, I can't imagine spending another minute of my life without you in it. I'm asking you to find it in your heart to forgive me and give me another chance at proving my love. Will you marry me and make it a lifetime chance?"

The way Susan saw it, she had two choices. She could pull him to his feet and accept, or she could fall to her own knees and accept. She opted for the latter.

"Yes," she told him, cupping his face in her hands and smothering him with kisses. "Yes, yes, yes!"

Susan had never known love to spin her round and round in such heady ecstasy. The thought of obtaining this man's forgiveness had been more than she had allowed herself to hope for. That he not only wanted her back in his bed but completely and openly in his life as his lawful wife was truly the stuff of the fairy tales that she had foresworn not so very long ago. Then again, not so long ago, she might have been caught foolishly trying to analyze happiness rather than simply cherishing it.

Susan was not about to make that mistake again. The only dark cloud left on the horizon was the fact that the real murderer had not been apprehended. With Sebastian officially exonerated, however, it was unlikely he would remain a target. Indeed, if love could conquer the impersonal machinations of the legal system, what chance had a mere human to come between them and happiness? Susan had to believe that someone who could outwit a pack of paid guerrillas could hold his own against some two-bit organizational mole. In any case, she wanted nothing more out of life than to face both its perils and its joys with the man she loved. It was time to accept that the nightmare was over, time to leave the rest of the investigation to the police, to a go-getter prosecutor with a grudge to settle and to Robert Cole, the private investigator whose gut feeling had told him something was amiss.

Before taking Susan home to Rosa and announcing their wedding plans to the world, Sebastian kissed her soundly once again. His lips were warm and sensual and full of promise. The promise of a future based on an unshakable foundation of trust and love—his best possible defense against a life of emptiness and deep regret. Losing the bet that he had posed to the bachelors of the Texas Cattleman's Club was the best thing to ever happen to him, Seb thought. When the time came, he would gladly raise his glass in a salute to the last bachelor standing, secure in the knowledge that a loving wife and the prospect of a house full of children truly made him the richest millionaire on the face of the earth.

* * * * *

Watch for the next installment of the

TEXAS CATTLEMAN'S CLUB:
THE LAST BACHELOR

*When Jason Windover—drop-dead
gorgeous cowboy and steadfast
bachelor—is assigned to keep an eye on
the feisty Meredith Silver, he never
expected to fall for her…literally. Can
this playboy convince Meredith to turn
their tumultuous relationship into a
permanent love match?*

THE PLAYBOY MEETS HIS MATCH

by Sara Orwig
*Coming to you from Silhouette Desire
in May 2002.*

*And now for a sneak preview of
THE PLAYBOY MEETS HIS MATCH,
please turn the page.*

One

"**D**on't tell me I'm the club expert at seduction," Jason Windover grumbled good-naturedly, glancing around the circle of friends and fellow members of the Texas Cattleman's Club as they sat in one of the elegant private meeting rooms. Thick carpets, dark paneling and polished wood flooring graced the spacious room built over ninety years earlier. A boar's head was mounted above the stone mantel, and a Tiffany chandelier glittered brightly.

The Texas Cattleman's Club was one of Texas's oldest and most exclusive clubs. It was a place where Jason usually could relax and enjoy his friends, but at the moment he was mildly annoyed. He crossed his jean-clad legs, resting one booted foot on his knee, and arched his brows.

"*Au contraire,*" Sebastian Wescott said, turning

to his longtime friend. "You're the one who excels at seduction, so I nominate you to get this Valkyrie out of our hair."

"I second that motion," snapped black-haired Will Bradford, a partner of Wescott Oil Enterprises.

Jason looked into Sebastian's silver-gray eyes and shook his head. "If nothing else, she's not my type," Jason said coolly, certain this foolishness would pass. "I like tall, long-legged, sophisticated blondes. Beautiful blondes who are poised and sexy. This wildcat sounds like five feet of pure trouble and anything but sophisticated, sexy or poised. Forget it, guys. It ain't gonna happen."

"The woman is unhinged. She belongs in a mental hospital," Dorian Brady added sharply. "She's got this vendetta against me—at the moment it's me. No telling who it will be tomorrow. She's mentally unstable, and her fixation could switch to any one of you. Lord knows, I haven't done the wild things she's accusing me of."

Studying Dorian, Jason felt cold distaste. Other than Dorian, Jason liked all the other members of the Texas Cattleman's Club, which was an exclusive, prestigious club that was a facade for the members to work together covertly on secret missions to save innocent lives. While most of the men had grown up in and around Royal, Texas, Dorian was a relative newcomer, yet related to Sebastian. There was an arrogance about Dorian that rankled him, but Jason knew he needed to get over his dislike. Dorian was, after all, Seb's half brother.

"You're elected," Rob Cole said dryly to Jason.

"You're the detective—you should know how to handle her."

"Nope. You have a way with women, and I already have my hands full with trying to find out what I can about our unsolved murder here in Royal." Rob studied the circle of men. "We have someone trying to frame Sebastian for the murder of Eric Chambers. We don't need this woman in our hair while we're trying to find out who's behind this."

"I wasn't here when she burst in on y'all, but I've heard what an unholy commotion she caused here at the club. Dammit, don't dump this on me." All of the men looked at Jason. "C'mon, y'all," Jason argued.

"You have to be the one," Sebastian replied. "You're the CIA trained operative, so you've dealt with difficult people before. Frankly, I've been through enough lately and I have a new bride to devote myself to."

Jason sighed and waved his hand. "Save your excuses. I can guess all of them. All right. I'll try to keep the little wildcat out of our hair."

"That problem solved, let's adjourn to poker," Keith, the computer expert, suggested, his brown eyes twinkling.

The men agreed swiftly, and Jason knew the matter was settled. Morosely, he joined them, getting a fresh drink, going through motions while he contemplated his assignment. He didn't like one thing about it. He was not accustomed to forcing a female to do something she didn't want to do—in this case, he was going to have to do exactly that in order to keep this little wildcat out of the other guys' ways.

Will, Rob and Sebastian were all recently married. It had become an epidemic, except he was safe—no marriage for him—at the moment there wasn't even a woman in his life. Maybe Keith should be the one to take care of this nuisance. Jason wondered whether Keith had ever gotten over his old flame, Andrea O'Rourke. He said he had, but he sure didn't act like it. Jason sighed. He could understand why this assignment had been dumped on him, but he didn't like it. Thank goodness he wasn't involved with anyone right now because this would be a very unwanted complication in his life. He wished he could just haul this woman down to jail and ask Sheriff Escobar to lock her up and throw away the key until all their mysteries were solved.

When Jason realized he was losing the first round of the poker game, he shifted his thoughts to cards and forgot about Meredith Silver, hoping she had left town and he would never have to deal with her.

It was almost midnight when Jason pocketed his winnings and told his friends good-bye. Stepping outside, he inhaled the cool May air. A silver moon hung in the inky sky while stars were blotted out by the lights of the parking lot. As he crossed the lot to his black pickup, Jason's boot heels scraped the asphalt. As he reached for the door handle of his pickup, he heard a faint sound behind him.

The hairs on the back of Jason's neck prickled, and he froze motionless beside his pickup. His experience in the CIA had trained him to be a keen observer, and he knew he had heard the scrape of a footstep on the asphalt.

Jason stood in a row of empty cars and pickups.

When he had walked from the clubhouse, there hadn't been another person in sight. In spite of the seemingly empty lot, Jason doubted he was alone in the parking lot. Should he look under the next car? he wondered, or would it be better to try to discover what the person intended? Jason pocketed his keys and headed casually back to the club.

He went though the front door, down a hallway past the cloakroom and restrooms, and cut through the giant kitchen, touching the brim of his Stetson with his finger in silent greeting to the skeleton cooking crew still on duty at this late hour. They were familiar with the members of the club, and none of them questioned his presence in the kitchen as he passed through and went out a side door. Glad now that he had worn a dark blue western shirt and his dark jeans, he moved stealthily even though he was wearing western boots. He paused, his gaze sweeping over the empty lot and then settling on the car parked next to his.

He knew whom it belonged to—Dorian. As he watched, a shadow separated itself from the darker ones around it. Jason focused on a black-clad figure who had slithered out from beneath Dorian's car and now knelt beside the back tire.

Silver glinted in the moonlight. There was a clunk and then a swift hiss of air. When the vandal moved to the front tire, Jason sprinted from his hiding place, determined to catch the rascal who was vandalizing club members' tires in their private parking lot.

Seeing Jason, the culprit dropped the knife and ran. Jason's long legs gave him the advantage, and he stretched out his stride. As they raced across the lot, Jason made a flying tackle, wrapping his arms around the miscreant's tiny waist.

"Gotcha!" he snapped triumphantly as they both went crashing to the asphalt.

The high yelp didn't indicate anything about the vandal, but the moment they landed on the asphalt, surprise rippled through Jason as he felt the soft, curvaceous body beneath his. A female! And then he guessed who it was. The crazy woman who was stalking his fellow club member, Dorian Brady—the wildcat who was his assignment.

* * * * *

You are invited to enter the exclusive, masculine world of the...

Silhouette Desire's powerful miniseries features five wealthy Texas bachelors—all members of the state's most prestigious club—who set out to uncover a traitor in their midst... and discover their true loves!

THE MILLIONAIRE'S PREGNANT BRIDE
by Dixie Browning
February 2002 (SD #1420)

HER LONE STAR PROTECTOR
by Peggy Moreland
March 2002 (SD #1426)

TALL, DARK...AND FRAMED?
by Cathleen Galitz
April 2002 (SD #1433)

THE PLAYBOY MEETS HIS MATCH
by Sara Orwig
May 2002 (SD #1438)

THE BACHELOR TAKES A WIFE
by Jackie Merritt
June 2002 (SD #1444)

Available at your favorite retail outlet.

Silhouette®
Where love comes alive™

Visit Silhouette at www.eHarlequin.com   SDTCC02

eHARLEQUIN.com

community | membership

buy books | authors | online reads | magazine | learn to write

magazine

♥ **quizzes**

Is he the one? What kind of lover are you? Visit the **Quizzes** area to find out!

♥ **recipes for romance**

Get scrumptious meal ideas with our **Recipes for Romance**.

♥ **romantic movies**

Peek at the **Romantic Movies** area to find Top 10 Flicks about First Love, ten Supersexy Movies, and more.

♥ **royal romance**

Get the latest scoop on your favorite royals in **Royal Romance**.

♥ **games**

Check out the **Games** pages to find a ton of interactive romantic fun!

♥ **romantic travel**

In need of a romantic rendezvous? Visit the **Romantic Travel** section for articles and guides.

♥ **lovescopes**

Are you two compatible? Click your way to the **Lovescopes** area to find out now!

Silhouette —

where love comes alive—online...

Visit us online at
www.eHarlequin.com

SINTMAG

If you enjoyed what you just read,
then we've got an offer you can't resist!

Take 2 bestselling
love stories FREE!

Plus get a FREE surprise gift!

Clip this page and mail it to Silhouette Reader Service™

IN U.S.A.
3010 Walden Ave.
P.O. Box 1867
Buffalo, N.Y. 14240-1867

IN CANADA
P.O. Box 609
Fort Erie, Ontario
L2A 5X3

YES! Please send me 2 free Silhouette Desire® novels and my free surprise gift. After receiving them, if I don't wish to receive anymore, I can return the shipping statement marked cancel. If I don't cancel, I will receive 6 brand-new novels every month, before they're available in stores! In the U.S.A., bill me at the bargain price of $3.34 plus 25¢ shipping and handling per book and applicable sales tax, if any*. In Canada, bill me at the bargain price of $3.74 plus 25¢ shipping and handling per book and applicable taxes**. That's the complete price and a savings of at least 10% off the cover prices—what a great deal! I understand that accepting the 2 free books and gift places me under no obligation ever to buy any books. I can always return a shipment and cancel at any time. Even if I never buy another book from Silhouette, the 2 free books and gift are mine to keep forever.

225 SEN DFNS
326 SEN DFNT

Name	(PLEASE PRINT)
Address	Apt.#
City	State/Prov. Zip/Postal Code

* Terms and prices subject to change without notice. Sales tax applicable in N.Y.
** Canadian residents will be charged applicable provincial taxes and GST.
All orders subject to approval. Offer limited to one per household and not valid to current Silhouette Desire® subscribers.
® are registered trademarks of Harlequin Enterprises Limited.

DES01   ©1998 Harlequin Enterprises Limited

Silhouette Books presents a dazzling keepsake collection featuring two full-length novels by international bestselling author

DIANA PALMER

Brides To Be

(On sale May 2002)

THE AUSTRALIAN
Will rugged outback rancher Jonathan Sterling be roped into marriage?

HEART OF ICE
Close proximity sparks a breathtaking attraction between a feisty young woman and a hardheaded bachelor!

You'll be swept off your feet by Diana Palmer's BRIDES TO BE.

Don't miss out on this special two-in-one volume, available soon.

Available only from Silhouette Books at your favorite retail outlet.

Where love comes alive™

Visit Silhouette at www.eHarlequin.com   PSBTB

ANN MAJOR
CHRISTINE RIMMER
BEVERLY BARTON

cordially invite you to attend the year's most exclusive party at the **LONE STAR COUNTRY CLUB!**

Meet three very different young women who'll discover that wishes *can* come true!

LONE STAR
COUNTRY CLUB:
The Debutantes

Lone Star Country Club:
Where Texas society reigns
supreme—and appearances
are *everything*.

Available in May
at your favorite retail outlet,
only from Silhouette.

Where love comes alive™

Visit Silhouette at www.eHarlequin.com   PSLSCCTD

Silhouette Desire

presents

DYNASTIES:
THE
CONNELLYS

A brand-new miniseries about the Connellys of Chicago,
a wealthy, powerful American family tied by blood to the
royal family of the island kingdom of Altaria.
They're wealthy, powerful and rocked by
scandal, betrayal…and passion!

Look for a whole year of glamorous and
utterly romantic tales in 2002:

January: **TALL, DARK & ROYAL** by Leanne Banks

February: **MATERNALLY YOURS** by Kathie DeNosky

March: **THE SHEIKH TAKES A BRIDE** by Caroline Cross

April: **THE SEAL'S SURRENDER** by Maureen Child

May: **PLAIN JANE & DOCTOR DAD** by Kate Little

June: **AND THE WINNER GETS…MARRIED!** by Metsy Hingle

July: **THE ROYAL & THE RUNAWAY BRIDE** by Kathryn Jensen

August: **HIS E-MAIL ORDER WIFE** by Kristi Gold

September: **THE SECRET BABY BOND** by Cindy Gerard

October: **CINDERELLA'S CONVENIENT HUSBAND**
by Katherine Garbera

November: **EXPECTING…AND IN DANGER** by Eileen Wilks

December: **CHEROKEE MARRIAGE DARE**
by Sheri WhiteFeather

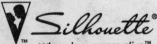

Silhouette

Where love comes alive™

Visit Silhouette at www.eHarlequin.com   SDDYN02